"It's impossible," Natalie said

"You must realize I couldn't work for you."

"Why?" Jake Lang's glance was cool and direct. "It's a chance in a million, and you know it."

It was true. Natalie sighed. "I'd have to think about it."

"You're very beautiful," he said, "and too young to bury yourself alive. Looking at you now I sometimes think I imagined the passionate woman I held in my arms that night."

"I wish you wouldn't talk about it," she said, flushing. "It's embarrassing."

"What happened that night is part of you, Natalie," Jake said firmly, "and you have to face it. You're trying to live in a vacuum. You've got to break out of it before it turns your warm blood to ice water and leaves you as dead as your husband."

Other titles by

CHARLOTTE LAMB
IN HARLEQUIN PRESENTS

Other titles by

CHARLOTTE LAMB
IN HARLEQUIN ROMANCES

Many of these titles, and other titles in the Harlequin Romance series, are available at your local bookseller. For a free catalogue listing all available Harlequin Presents and Harlequin Romances, send your name and address to:

HARLEQUIN READER SERVICE,
M.P.O. Box 707,
Niagara Falls, N.Y. 14302
Canadian address:
Stratford, Ontario, Canada N5A 6W2

CHARLOTTE LAMB

frustration

Harlequin Books

TORONTO · LONDON · NEW YORK · AMSTERDAM
SYDNEY · HAMBURG · PARIS · STOCKHOLM

Harlequin Presents edition published February 1980
ISBN 0-373-10339-5

Original hardcover edition published in 1979
by Mills & Boon Limited

CHAPTER ONE

IT was during the coffee break that Natalie realised she had lost her wedding ring. She reached out to pass the sugar bowl to Carol and her hand stayed fixed in position while Carol gazed at her blankly and she looked at that bare left hand with horror-stricken eyes.

'What's wrong?' Carol leaned over and took the sugar bowl firmly, then placed it on the table. Her neat-featured face showed distress as she took in Natalie's irrepressible tears. 'Natalie! For heaven's sake!'

'My ring,' Natalie got out thickly.

Carol glanced down. Her eyes reflected shock. 'Oh, no, you poor girl!' She put her hand down over Natalie's and patted her gently. 'Don't panic. Think. Where did you last see it? Did you take it off when you washed this morning? Do you remember seeing it then?'

Natalie could not remember anything. Her mind was a blank. She could not recall a second of the day's events. Nothing that had happened to her, nothing she had done, had made any impression because her mind was so totally occupied with thoughts of Angus. He had walked through her head all day. Their second wedding anniversary, a day which should have been radiant, as their wedding day had been, even though it had been a day of sun and showers alternately, keeping her in suspense right up to the moment she stepped out of the white-ribboned wedding car on her father's arm and saw the sun break brilliantly through the fluffy clouds. Dad had looked up and grinned at her sideways. 'Just for you,' he had whispered, and she had been smiling as she walked down the aisle towards Angus.

'Take it step by step,' Carol suggested patiently. 'You must have noticed it at some time in the morning.'

She had noticed the sun glinting on her wedding photograph as she got a book from the bookcase. For a second her body had shivered as though pierced by a sliver of ice, then she had averted her eyes and turned away. Today was going to be hard enough to bear without that memory to haunt her.

'When you were typing,' Carol suggested, watching her, the rather deep-set brown eyes kind. 'Did you look down and see it then at any time?'

Natalie shook her head dumbly. Even if she had looked she would not have seen anything. Angus's face had come between her and every object she saw, his smiling grey eyes mirrored in windows, his dark hair lined in every moving shadow. Impossible, she thought. How was it possible, believable, that he had been dead just over a year? Her first wedding anniversary had passed without notice. She had been too ill to realise what day it was and nobody had wanted to remind her.

'I expect it's safe at home,' Carol said, still trying to reach her. 'In the bathroom or the bedroom— that's usually where rings get lost. When you got ready this morning you probably took it off.'

'Yes, probably,' said Natalie, realising with a start

that she was distressing her and sorry for it. She pulled herself together with an effort and smiled tremulously, pushing a hand through her long black hair. She had not had it cut for months. It had grown and grown until now it hung down her back in a full sleek swathe. It needed to be thinned, she thought, and trimmed back to some sort of style, but she had not felt like making the effort.

Carol gave her a shrewd glance. 'What are you doing tonight?'

Blankly, Natalie shrugged. 'Going back to the apartment, I suppose.' What else did she ever do? She had not been out for weeks. Now and then she visited her family. Her parents lived at Weymouth on the Dorset coast in a little house which looked down on the half-moon of the bay, their view of the sea the main attraction when they bought the place. It was a long journey by train and she did not own a car. Her visits were not frequent, but she wrote every week, although no doubt the letters were scrappy and dull; she had nothing to say to them. She sat sometimes and dredged her mind helplessly for something, anything to say. It would be dull for them to read: 'I'm desperately unhappy, oh, God, I wish I'd died with him.' That would be boring. It would upset them and there was nothing they could do.

Even less frequently she visited Angus's parents. Twice in the last year she had gone up to Scotland to see them and each time it had been agony, but she had gone, and his mother had been so appallingly brave it had made everything worse. Because Natalie knew how much Angus had been loved, not only by herself, but by his parents. He had been their only son, adored and needed, which made his death even less bearable.

The only frequent visits she made were to her sister Angela, who was married with two small toddlers. Angela was brisk and matter-of-fact. She was Natalie's lifeline. When she was there she got no tears, no comfort. Angela bullied her. 'Do the washing up while I wash Colin's ears. Good heavens, girl, is that how you peel potatoes? They're half peel!' It helped. It made things feel more normal.

'Natalie, wake up!' Carol said on a rough sigh, and she gave her an apologetic look. Since she came to work at Metropolis TV she had made friends with several of the other secretaries, but Carol was the nicest of them. She valued her friendship.

'I'm sorry, I'm being a bore,' she said, then on a deep breath, 'You see, it's my wedding anniversary.'

Carol inhaled sharply. 'No! Oh, Natalie, I am sorry. How awful, to lose your ring today of all days!'

Natalie looked down at her left hand wryly. 'It's my fault. I've lost a lot of weight. I meant to have the ring altered, made smaller, but I kept putting it off.' Good intentions were always too late in being kept. 'I expect it just slid off and I never noticed.'

Carol inspected her with interest. 'Your figure is just a tiny bit thin, but you still look fantastic. I envy you your height. I wish I was taller.'

Carol was five foot two and slightly plump, although her figure had a certain rounded appeal which had not gone unnoticed. Natalie gave her a quick smile. 'You're fine as you are. Very pocket Venus.'

Carol laughed, catching her lower lip between her teeth. She had a neat round head of warm brown hair the colour of teak, her features nicely proportioned, her smile quick and impulsive. The men who worked in the department noticed her and smiled back a good deal, but Carol had no special boy-friend. She was three years younger than Natalie, who was twenty-four, and Carol was in no hurry to settle down. She loved her job. She felt lucky to have it. It was glamorous, busy and exciting.

'Why don't you come with me tonight?' Carol asked suddenly. 'It would be better for you than going back to an empty flat and brooding all evening.'

'What?' Blinking, Natalie looked at her. 'I'm sorry, I don't follow.'

'The party,' Carol urged.

Natalie had forgotten hearing her mention the party she was going to that night and now she grimaced, knowing she had never felt less like going to a party in her life. 'It's kind of you, but no, I don't think so.'

'You should,' Carol insisted firmly. 'Look, you've worked here for nine months and in that time you've never been to one of our parties. Isn't it time you started joining in? Met people socially instead of just at the office? We're a pretty social crowd, you know. There's something going on all the time.'

'I had gathered that,' Natalie admitted, smiling. There were a large number of unattached people in the department. They all lived in apartments or bedsitting-rooms in London, usually far from their family homes, and they tended to see each other outside working hours as well as during them. She had vaguely noticed activity of that kind going on around her, but she had never felt any interest. When she first arrived several of the men had asked her out, but she had refused coolly. They all knew she was recently widowed. How, she wasn't sure, she had never told any of them, but it was like that here. News spread like wildfire through the grapevine. People just seemed to know everything about you.

Carol had a mulish look. 'You're coming,' she said, setting her pretty pink mouth. 'It's settled. I won't take no for an answer.'

'Perhaps some other night,' Natalie prevaricated. Not tonight. She could not go out and pretend to enjoy a party tonight.

'Don't argue,' Carol told her. 'I'm not going to have my evening ruined by imagining you sitting in an empty apartment brooding yourself sick.'

Natalie flushed and looked at her with a wince. 'I'm sorry if anything I've said could do that ...'

'Oh, no,' Carol said quickly, 'it's me who's sorry. I shouldn't have said that, but do come. Even if it's just for an hour, to pop in and say hello to everybody? I think you need to break out of your shell, and now is as good a time as any.'

Carol was not the first person to speak sharply to her on this subject, but it had stung just now. Brooding herself sick! It sounded like an accusation of self-pity, and maybe that was what she had been doing for months, pitying herself. Angela had said something very similar a week ago, looking at her with critical bright eyes. 'Snap out of it,' she had commanded. 'Do you think Angus would have wanted to see you like this? Where's your backbone? It's time you faced facts. You're alive, Nat, and Angus isn't. It may hurt, but it's a fact.'

Then she had looked at her sister with something approaching hatred and flung off in a cold temper.

But now she drew a long breath.

'I'm not dressed for a party.' She knew it began at around eight and she was working until seven. There would be no time to go home and change.

'Buy a new dress,' said Carol, face brightening. 'Tell you what, I'll come with you—I love choosing clothes for other people. We'll go in the lunch hour.'

Metropolis TV was housed in a new white office block in the centre of London. The building had been erected by a large property firm who had had trouble finding a tenant for the place. When Metropolis took on the lease, the employees took to calling the building The Elephant because the owners had found it a white elephant on their hands for several years. The office planning had been very progressive. Huge open office floors which were noisy and bright and spacious had defects which were gradually becoming overwhelmingly apparent. There was no privacy. It was hard to concentrate with so much going on around one. There was continual movement, constant noise. Already there were plans for alterations, the partition of parts of the offices, but so far ideas were in the planning stage, and the staff suffered, although not in silence. When two or three were gathered together the complaints were unceasing.

Returning to her desk in the centre of one of the floors, Natalie forced her mind back to her work. She was typing a script for Jake Lang, one of the better known of the producers. It was fascinating stuff and she would normally have been very interested in it, but today she was finding it difficult to concentrate. She wore headphones, since she was typing from an audio machine, and it made her jump when Carol lifted one of the earpieces and asked: 'Coming to lunch?'

Looking in amazement at the huge white office clock, she nodded. Had the time gone so fast? She switched off the machine and the deep, cool voice to which she had been listening stopped dead. Carol peered over her shoulder. 'What's that?'

'The new Lang scripts. I've been detailed to do the lot.'

'You haven't? Lucky beast. Oh, what I'd give to work for him!' Carol rolled her brown eyes expressively, grinning. 'He got back last week, Sandra says. She saw him in the lift, looking as brown as a berry and sexier than ever.'

Natalie barely heard her. She was carefully sliding the typed sheets into the folder and locking it away in her top drawer. Carol stared.

'Why are you doing that?'

'He put a note in with the tapes asking for great security. He doesn't want anyone to see the scripts before transmission.'

Carol looked fascinated. 'Perhaps he's found King Solomon's Mines.'

Jake Lang had been in Africa for two years with a camera team filming the history of the development of the continent from the early days of Arab infiltration, and there was enormous curiosity in the media about the programmes he was planning on the subject. His previous two series had been hugely popular, but rumour had it that the third was going to break all records. Already a number of foreign TV companies had begun bidding for the rights to it. Jake Lang had had offers from American companies to go over there to work, but as far as was known he had refused them.

Although Natalie had been immersed in her own

affairs while she typed the script she had not been unaware of the quality of the stuff she was transcribing. It was too good to be missed, and the voice speaking had been an odd mixture of controlled authority and husky sensuality, indicating a man who knew what he wanted and went for it without allowing anything to get in the way.

Following Carol along the corridor to the lift, she dismissed Jake Lang from her mind without trouble and made herself dwell on the idea of buying a new dress. Carol was talking excitedly. 'Something bright and sexy,' she suggested. 'Red. Now you can wear red.'

But when they stood in the dress shop five minutes' walk from their office, Natalie at once saw the very dress she knew she wanted, and it was not red. Carol shook her head. 'Not blue,' she disapproved. 'The wrong colour in your mood.'

It was not blue, Natalie thought. It was a mixture of green and blue, a strange beautiful shade, lustrous and cool, like Mediterranean waters in sunlight.

Even Carol had to admit it looked good when Natalie emerged from the fitting room. She whistled softly. 'You'll knock their eyes out!'

They went straight from the office to the party. Changing in the cloakroom was fun. There were several other girls going and they giggled a lot, admiring each other's clothes, swopping perfumes and jewellery. When Natalie walked out to join them they all stared. She had never taken so much trouble with her appearance since she joined the firm and she was pleased with their expressions.

In the mirror she saw a tall, slender girl with shining black hair which fell in soft waves down

her back, her dress reflecting the light like the sea
on a summer day, her shoulders and throat bare, the
silken bodice cupping her high breasts, curving
over her waist and out into a stiff swishing skirt
which flared as she walked.

'Unfair competition,' said Sandra, who worked in
the same office. She grinned to show it was a joke,
but her pale blue eyes were regretful.

'What's the perfume?' Carol asked, sniffing
thoughtfully.

'Chanel,' said Natalie, and their eyebrows flew
up.

'Extravagant girl! Did you buy it?'

'Yes,' she said. It had been a sudden whim as she
passed the perfume counter. Angus had bought her
Chanel for her birthday during their engagement.
It had been his favourite perfume.

Sandra made a little face, an acquisitive look in
her eyes. 'Can I ...' she began, and Carol cut in
sharply.

'No. It suits Natalie, but you're already wearing
something pretty explosive. Do you want to smell
like a perfume counter?'

Sandra shrugged crossly. Although she was not
unfriendly she was inclined to covet things; clothes,
jewellery, other girls' men, and when she wanted
something she abandoned everything in her pursuit
of it. Her pale eyes glinted as she looked Natalie up
and down. Carol sensed an unkindness on her
tongue and hurriedly suggested it was time they
left.

'We don't want to be too late or all the food will
have vanished. Rob said he was getting caviar, but
that will go first.'

It was Rob's birthday and his small apartment was

packed with people. The music drummed fiercely, making the rooms seem smaller than ever, especially with so many people packed into them. They spilled over into bathroom and kitchen. They leaned on the walls in the narrow hall. Rob had cunningly invited all his neighbours so that nobody should complain about the noise and there was no effort to turn down the stereo equipment. It blared through the whole building.

Natalie had eaten bits of curried fish, scraps of ham curled with pineapple on sticks, tiny canapés and a few crisps, but Carol's warning that the food would vanish had proved accurate. There was barely enough for half the number of people who had turned up. Still, there was plenty to drink, Rob said gaily, grinning at the girls. Natalie had been welcomed with interest and enthusiasm, a glass forced into her hand. Although she did not like drinking she found her glass being refilled every time she sipped it and with so little food in her stomach she was beginning to feel slightly drunk.

She danced with some of the men and parried their flirtatious remarks, evaded direct requests for a date, smiled at their corny jokes. Somewhere in the crush she lost all sight of Carol. The other girls had dived off as soon as they arrived. She saw Sandra dancing vigorously while she talked non-stop to a thin young man with curly brown hair who looked longingly at the door but did not have the courage to escape.

It was growing smokier and warmer by the minute. She excused herself to her current partner and pushed her way through the chattering throng by the door. Some thoughtful soul had opened the apartment front door. A cool gale blew through the hall and there was a small free space where she could breathe, turning to glance back into the room, one hand pushing back the dark cloud of her hair. Joe Hertley, one of the floormen, leant over and snapped off the main lights, leaving the room in shaded dimness. 'Great thinking, Joe,' someone called, and everyone laughed. Then someone else changed the vigorous blare for a slow, romantic tape to which the dancers drifted cheek to cheek.

The atmosphere of the whole party had changed. The talking grew muted or went on in outer rooms. Natalie shivered, feeling cold and alone. Time to go, she thought bleakly. She could not take this.

She glanced around for Carol to say goodbye to her and then it happened. On the other side of the room she saw a dark head and her heart plunged as though she were in a lift which had suddenly gone down. The texture and colour of the thick black hair, the strong moulding of the skull at the back, the uplift of the neck, were all exactly like Angus's. She stared incredulously and for one minute it just might have been true. Even the lean tall body, lounging casually as he talked to someone. Only the choice of clothes made it obvious. Angus would never have been seen dead in tight black jeans and a rollneck grey shirt. He always wore formal suits, immaculate and elegant.

Even so she waited, her eyes on that head, begging him silently to turn so that she could see his face.

Of course he would not look anything like Angus. But she couldn't tear herself away until she saw him.

Perhaps her intense concentration on him got through to him somehow. Suddenly she saw him straighten, the muscles visible beneath his figure-hugging shirt tightening. He turned his head and flicked a glance across the room. Even in profile he had a faint resemblance, but then he focussed on her, and it was over. He did not look like Angus at all.

Natalie was so disappointed that she only stood there, staring back at him; unconscious of herself, a slender seductive figure in shimmering sea-green, her pale throat beating with disturbed pulses, her eyes very wide and startled.

It seemed an eternity to her as she looked at him, taking in the strong, fierce lines of his face, his narrowing grey eyes and well-cut, sensual mouth, revising her first impression as she took in the nature revealed in his bones. He might not resemble Angus facially, but there was still that tantalising, bewildering resemblance.

Suddenly realising how she was staring, she flushed, looking away, and turned to leave. She would explain to Carol tomorrow, she thought.

A hand touched her arm. She looked round, her breath stopping as she saw who stood beside her.

'Hallo,' he said in tones of intimacy, as though they had known each other all their lives, as though he had been waiting for her to come.

Taken aback, she blushed, the colour running up her slender neck to her face in a warm tide. The grey eyes watched it flowing under her skin as intently as though he were fascinated.

'Hallo,' she answered huskily. What on earth must he be thinking?

'Dance with me,' he invited, smiling into her lifted eyes.

She began to stammer some sort of excuse, looking away, but he smiled, putting a finger on her lips, and his arm slid around her. She tensed at that first touch, shooting a look upwards at him, and felt him watching her. Then she knew she was not going to leave. And knew that he was confident of it, too.

They seemed to drift into the music, their bodies close, his arms wrapped around her possessively, one hand at her waist, the other beginning to move slowly, stroking her back, following the elegant line of her spine, moving up to fondle the soft roundness of her shoulder.

She was in a dream. She danced, eyes closed, her cheek laid against his, contentedly aware of the hardness of bone and taut skin against her, the music whispering in her head. The smoky shadows flowed around them, and some were people, but she never saw them. Her head was light, cloudy, and her arms were now clinging round his neck. She did not even remember how they got there.

'My God, you're beautiful,' he whispered against her ear, and his mouth moved gently over the pale, spiralled shell of it, brushing light kisses on the lobe and then behind the ear, his face in the drifting strands of her hair.

She didn't speak. The thick black hair was under her fingers. She touched it passionately, stroking the strong nape of his neck, unaware of anything but the dream enfolding her. Angus, she thought, Angus.

There was a hand sliding along her collarbone. It stroked her throat and took her chin gently, turning her head. Eyes closed, she felt a mouth touch her lips and groaned.

'Let's get out of here,' he muttered with a strange

burning inflection, standing still. Natalie blinked, eyes opening reluctantly.

The room swam out of the shadows and now some of the shadows had faces which were staring at them. Some were curious, others amused, and one held distinct annoyance. Sandra's cross little eyes looked daggers, but Natalie dreamily glanced away without a flicker, barely knowing who anyone was at this moment.

'Coming?' he asked, watching her, and she looked at him through her lashes and smiled, unaware that that slow smile held explicit invitation, a sensuous awareness which glimmered in her eyes.

He drew a strange deep breath. 'Got a coat?' he asked, his voice rough, as though he was finding it hard to speak at all, and she felt the same. She could not answer. She only shook her head.

Then they were fighting their way out of the room, followed by speculative eyes, the insidious sweetness of the music lilting through her mind as she felt his arm close round her to guide her through the front door.

The night air was cold and made her gasp, penetrating the mistiness of her brain.

'My car's over here,' he said beside her.

Had she walked far in the invigorating wind she might have woken up, but the drink she had consumed on an almost empty stomach had a strong grip on her, and in another moment she was in his car, and snuggling down into the warmth his heater provided as they drove away.

He glanced down at the fine strands of hair clinging to his sleeve as her head lay against him and smiled. 'You must be the least talkative woman I've ever met.'

'I'm sorry,' she said, glancing up.

'Don't be,' he said. 'I like it.' The grey eyes lingered on her face. In profile he almost could be Angus. He had those strong features, the fleshless strength which had made Angus a formidable rugger player, and something about him suggested that he possessed Angus's driving energy too, his ambition and personal dynamism.

'Where do you live?' he asked, and she told him, leaning back with closed eyes as he drove through the empty streets. The car drew up and she got out in the same daze. 'Coffee?' he suggested, following her.

She looked round as if surprised to find him standing next to her, then smiled. After the street, her flat was warm and welcoming. He followed her into the kitchen, but as she moved to get down the percolator his arms slid round her body, pulling her back against him.

His mouth moved on her neck and she could feel tension in the lean body behind her. 'I thought it only happened in dreams,' he whispered on her skin. 'Are you a dream? You're too beautiful to be real.'

She closed her eyes. Yes, she thought, it is a dream, and I've dreamt like this before, but it was never so piercingly sweet. She had no premonition of consequence, no comprehension of any reality outside what was happening inside her.

He turned her into his arms and his mouth came down in a seeking movement. Her arms went round his neck, fingers thrusting into the familiar thick hair. Her heart began beating wildly. They kissed as though they were lovers parted for years and at last united.

She heard the deep beat of his heart against her breasts, the warmth of his flesh passing into her own. He pulled her closer, his hands moving restlessly over her body. 'If I'm dreaming this I hope I never wake,' he muttered, his mouth moving down to her throat. She lay in his strong arms, her head tilted back, allowing him to graze over her skin, his lips gliding from neck to shoulder and down to the delicate white glimmer of her high breasts. He began to shake. She felt his convulsive movements and moaned, then his mouth closed on hers again and the kiss became deep, deeper, until they were both breathless and dazed.

'The coffee,' she whispered, her eyes lowered, terrified to look at him. She had never behaved like this with a stranger before in her life. Even with Angus it had been weeks before he kissed her. She was normally a shy, quiet girl, very slightly withdrawn, her manner cool enough to keep men at their distance while she made up her mind about them.

Since Angus died she had not made any dates or let any other man get close enough to touch her. She had lived in a cold shell of misery, but now, tonight, the shell had broken open and she was shuddering in a realisation of her own vulnerability.

'It isn't coffee I want,' he said roughly, his voice husky too. He put his hand against her throat, caressing her skin. 'Don't you know that? Of course you do.'

She backed, her hands against his hard shoulders. The black lashes flickered upward and her wide blue eyes stared at him, their expression alarmed and yet still molten with sensual feeling. 'No,' she said faintly, her lips trembling.

His hands closed over her own, lifted them. He kissed the cool palms gently, looking at her with a strangely intimate smile. 'Okay, we've skipped a few places, but we're here now and we both know it. It's been like that from the first look. I wanted you on sight and if you're honest you felt the same.'

Her head was throbbing with a strange fever, her eyes were glazed and her mouth dry. She tried to speak, to deny, but she couldn't force out a syllable. Her eyes dropped to his mouth and he bent forward slowly, the hard, sensual line holding her as it came nearer until it touched her and she groaned, her head falling back, her mouth opening.

His mouth still kissing her hotly, he lifted her into his arms and carried her down the short corridor, kicking open the bedroom door. She tried to struggle out of her tranced state as she felt his hands on her zip, and he kissed her again. 'Don't try to think. Go with the tide.'

The tide ran strongly. The darkness made it easier because under her fingers his bones were poignantly familiar, and her unfed sensual hunger flamed too urgently for her to resist. He was an unhurried, gentle lover, the stroke of his hands on her skin almost an act of love in itself, as though touching her sent him crazy. She was moaning now, twisting closer, the naked brush of skin on skin making her feverish.

Suddenly he lay still, staring at her through the dark. 'What the hell did you just call me?'

She did not want to be drawn out of the warm ocean tide of passion flowing in her blood. 'What?' she stammered.

'Who's Angus?' he asked harshly.

The question was a knife thrust deep into her

flesh. 'Oh, God!' she moaned, turning her face away.

He pulled her head round violently. 'I asked you a question!'

She had begun to cry silently, covering her face.

'Who's Angus?' he asked again, and now there was a note in his voice which terrified her.

'My husband,' she whispered.

'God,' he said hoarsely, then he was off the bed and dressing in the darkness, finding his clothes in disarray on the floor, putting them on with efficient, terse movements which, although she could barely see his face, very clearly indicated his anger.

Natalie lay there, so shocked she was unaware of her nakedness, her mind and body stone cold, feeling sick, bitterly accusing herself. She could hear the little silver bedside clock which Angus had given her at their wedding ticking quickly, lightly, like a little voice, and it accused her too.

He turned, fully dressed, and she felt him staring down at her through the darkness. The pale steely glint of his eyes moved down the glimmer of her body and although their expression was invisible to her she sensed the contemptuous distaste in that look.

'Thank Angus for the loan of his property,' he said caustically. 'But tell him I never have liked getting second-hand goods, however cheap, and he has my sympathy.'

The door had slammed before she was over the shock of the biting words and tone. She had no chance to apologise, explain. His footsteps thudded along the corridor, the front door crashed open and shut, the glass in every room rattling in protest as he slammed it.

Natalie turned her face into the pillow and cried until, exhausted, she fell asleep. For the first time in a year she did not dream of Angus, but her sleep was not easy. She tossed and turned, mumbling, and when she woke at dawn she was burning with feverish heat. For a moment she lay there, puzzled, realising she had slept without a stitch of clothing, and wondered why, but then it came back to her and her face contracted in a groan of pain.

What on earth had got into her? She had not even asked his name or told him hers. She had practically begged him to behave the way he had. She could not blame him. What would any man think if a young woman acted the way she had done last night? She had been offering herself to him from the moment they met. No doubt he now thought it was something she did all the time.

God, I hope I never set eyes on him again, she thought. He can't be someone from the firm. I'd have seen him, caught that faint resemblance to Angus before. He must be someone's friend, one of those stray guests every party collects.

It was no comfort to put the blame on the unusual amount of drink she had taken at the party. Drink and the collective result of months of lonely unhappiness might explain, but they could not excuse the way she had acted. It was out of character, shameful, and Natalie wished she had never gone to that party.

CHAPTER TWO

SHE was late arriving at the office and the enormous room was already throbbing with noise and the clatter of machines. She walked up the aisle in which her desk lay, aware of the fixed stares riveted on her back, yet keeping her head held high and hoping the faint flush on her face would be taken for the result of a dash to get to work in cold weather.

Carol was gazing at her oddly as she sat down and stripped the cover from her machine. Natalie avoided her eyes, picking up the headphones and placing them over her ears, switching on so that the deep cool voice could resume, but even as she did so someone touched her arm, and she switched off again reluctantly, glancing round.

It was the supervisor, Mrs Dawkins, looking flustered. She was a rawboned woman of fifty or so, her skin extremely clear and smooth for her age, but her eyes always worried as though invisible disaster stalked her from morning to night.

'Yes, Mrs Dawkins?' Natalie asked politely.

'Mrs Buchan, I'm sorry to disturb your work, but those tapes you're doing—well, how was I to know? There was no need to shout at me, I'm sure, but some of these men think they're a close relation to God! I had to hold the phone away from my ear. No need to shout, I told him, and he just shouted even more. I know it's a nuisance, but I suppose we'll have to do as he says.'

Patiently Natalie tried to unravel the core of her monologue. 'Do you mean something is wrong with the tapes?'

'Well, I suppose so, but he didn't say.'

Suppressing a sigh, Natalie tried again. 'What did he say exactly? What does he want done with them?'

Mrs Dawkins clicked her tongue. 'Stupid, aren't I? Didn't I say? Wants them in cutting room two right away—well, I think he said tapes 2 and 3, or was it 3 and 4? Anyway, right away, he said.' She gazed at Natalie wistfully. 'If you don't mind, dear.'

There seemed little point in minding. Natalie got up and gathered the tapes together and walked up the aisle again. There was a distinct whisper running behind her as she passed, but she ignored it, her lids down over her deep blue eyes. There was going to be gossip for some time, she saw that; Sandra would make certain of it. Natalie would have to ride out the storm, however embarrassing the consequences of that one night's madness.

Carol had looked at her reproachfully when she did not pause to speak to her. No doubt she was dying to ask her questions. Carol loved hearing the details of everyone's love life and Natalie dreaded the moment when she finally had to face Carol and refuse to admit anything.

As she got into the lift to go down to cutting room 2 the wind blew through an open window and a speck of dust flew into her eye. She stood in the lift searching in her bag for a handkerchief, her eye watering. Her fingers closed on something cold and smooth and her heart missed a beat. She pulled it out and looked at it, whitening. Her wedding ring.

If she had never lost it, she thought, she would not have gone to that party.

She slid it on to her finger and lifted it to her cheek, sighing. Oh, well, she had it back, thank God. That was one small comfort. It had been eating at her mind to have lost it, her last real link with Angus.

The lift stopped dead with a shudder and she watched the door open. The cutting rooms lay in the basement below ground level, windowless, brilliantly lighted and silent. She stepped out of the lift and glanced down the row of portholed doors. Number 2 was on the left. She pushed it open and found herself in darkness, a light flickering in a whitey grey stream across the room.

'Mr Lang?' she asked into the dark.

'Hmm?' The answer came from somewhere at the back of the room and she turned towards it.

'I'm Mrs Buchan from the script pool. You asked for the tapes of your series.'

There was a silence which struck her oddly. She moved an inch or two, peering into the dark, and the flickering light outlined her for a moment before she shifted away from it. 'Shall I leave them on a chair?' There did not seem to be anywhere else to put them.

She sensed but did not see a movement. The light was suddenly switched on and she turned, blinking, dazzled.

The shock of recognition was a physical pain. 'Oh, no!' she gasped, releasing her hold on the tapes.

He moved swiftly to catch them before they hit the ground. 'You damned little bitch,' he muttered. 'Those things are irreplaceable!'

Blindly she turned towards the door, knowing only that she had to get away from him. Why did it have to be him?

He put down the tapes and came after her, catching her arm before she could get out of the door. 'Oh, no, you don't,' he grated, dragging her back into the room with a violence which only just stopped short of open savagery.

She threw back her head in a defiant movement fuelled by sheer desperation, her long black hair flowing over her slender shoulders, the deep blue eyes meeting his cold glare head on and never wavering.

'So,' he said, 'your name is Buchan.' She knew now why his voice was so familiar to her. Why hadn't she realised last night? She had been sitting in the office listening to him all day, mesmerised by those deep tones.

His narrowed, icy eyes ran down over her in a comprehensive, scathing glance which made her feel sick. 'What is he? A man whose job takes him away for weeks on end, I suppose? While you amuse yourself in other men's arms.'

Her colour deepened but her eyes stayed steady, the merest flicker of the long lashes betraying her reaction to that insult. 'Look, I would have explained last night,' she began huskily, moistening her dry lips.

'Don't bother,' he cut in derisively. 'It was obvious.'

She stared at his hard, contemptuous face and was angry. 'Nothing is obvious, Mr Lang. I'd have thought at your age you would have learnt that much.'

'There are a lot of things I thought I'd learnt,'

he retorted. 'For instance, I believed I was too clever to get caught by a two-timing little bitch like you.' His mouth writhed in a horrible mimicry of amusement which held no real humour. 'God, was I wrong?' He looked her up and down again, every line of his face insulting her. 'What a fool you made of me last night! You must have laughed yourself sick.'

Natalie felt her anger leak away in a useless regret. 'I'm sorry,' she said gently.

His mouth tightened and the grey eyes sliced into her viciously. 'And that soft, cool little voice added to the whole damned fraud. Are you an actress, by any chance?'

'I told you, I'm from Scripts. I'm a secretary,' she said, wishing she could think of something to say to take the ice from his eyes.

There was a brief, strange silence. He looked away from her face, his cheekbones taut, his eyes half-veiled by his lids. 'Why did you call me that last night?'

'I'm sorry,' she said again, her voice distressed.

He shot her a quick look. 'Why?' he asked brusquely.

She drew a shaky breath. 'You look like him.'

He inhaled sharply, his whole body growing tense. She could feel the anger in him and stared at the floor.

'Is that why you were staring at me at the party?'

'Yes,' she whispered.

'Why you let me take you home, let me make love to you?' He was biting the words out as if the taste of them sickened him.

'Yes,' she whispered so faintly he had to bend to hear her.

'I see,' he said tightly, then he pushed her towards the door. 'Get out of here before I do something I'll regret.'

Natalie fled without waiting to hear more. She went to the cloakroom to wash her hot face and then went into the office. Carol gave her a speaking look, almost pleading, and she halted by her desk, smiling in a brittle fashion which hid the deep disturbance of her thoughts.

'What happened last night?' Carol hissed at once, without waiting to pretend she had anything else to say. 'Sandra says you went off with Jake Lang.'

'He did drive me home,' Natalie agreed quietly, keeping her eyes steady on Carol's face.

'And?' Carol gasped, eyes huge.

Natalie looked blankly at her. 'And what?'

'Oh, come on,' Carol said almost irately. 'Sandra says you were dancing with him in a real dream. Cheek to cheek, she said, right from the word go. Don't tell me he just went home and left you with a polite goodnight?'

Natalie felt colour stealing into her face. Angrily she said, 'As Sandra seems to have said so much, maybe she also knows the answer to that.'

She walked back to her desk with her head high. She had forgotten whose voice she would hear when she switched on the machine and it made her heart turn over to hear those cool, confident tones again. They held bitter memories for her now. They always would. She was shamed and furious with herself all over again. But her fingers went on typing and she did not look up to catch any more meaning looks.

Over coffee Carol looked at her with that reproachful gaze. 'What's wrong with a few interested questions? Look, in case you just hadn't heard, Jake Lang has been number one target for every girl in the office ever since he got back from Africa, yet you walk right in and lift him from under their noses after months of pretty standoffish behaviour. How do you expect us all to feel? I for one am dying of curiosity. Be a pal—give!'

Natalie was forced to smile. 'There's nothing to tell. We danced one dance, then he drove me home because I was tired.'

'One dance?' Carol's pencilled eyebrows rose comically. 'Come off it! Sandra says you kept going round and round holding on to each other as if you were drowning.'

Natalie flushed, looking away. Yes, perhaps it had looked like that. It had certainly felt like it. She felt a peculiar shiver run down her spine at the memory of those minutes in the smoky room while Jake Lang held her in his arms and brushed his lips over her cheek, her hair, her lips.

'We barely spoke to each other,' she said desperately.

'That figures,' said Carol, grinning, and suddenly Natalie laughed too, seeing the impish amusement in her eyes.

'Yes, well——' she murmured.

'Very revealing,' Carol teased. 'Did he kiss you?'

Did he! thought Natalie. She would hate Carol to even suspect how far it had gone. Aloud, she said, 'What sort of reputation have I got, for heaven's sake?'

Carol caught the tearless glitter of her eyes and sobered.

'Oh, Natalie, I'm sorry. I forgot Angus, I really did for a moment. It was just that everyone has been

talking about it this morning. Sandra was spilling
beans all over the office. And I didn't know a thing
about what happened. I suppose I was cross because they all expected me to know the inside story
and I felt a fool. They took it for granted that you'd
tell me about it.'

'Nothing *to* tell,' Natalie said lightly but firmly.

Carol eyed her hopefully, the brown eyes like a
hungry bird's. 'Not even whether you fancy him?
You must admit, Jake Lang is quite a prize for any
of us.'

'Jake Lang leaves me cold,' Natalie said on a
sharp note, and far too loudly in her irritation. A
hush fell on the canteen. Heads around them turned
and eyes stared. She pushed away her coffee cup
and stood up. As she hurried out of the clinical
white-walled room she felt herself under close observation. Well, she thought, that should settle it,
anyway. They can't think I didn't mean that.

At lunchtime she avoided Carol and had a sand-
wich in the nearby park, feeding most of it to the
sparrows which hopped and chirped on the asphalt
paths. The morning was bright and cool, a spring
morning, with clouds passing over the blue sky all
the time and the grass already pierced with the
yellow trumpets of daffodils. People walked past all
the time, many of the men glancing more than once
at the slender black-haired girl seated alone on the
park bench, her blue sweater and straight black
skirt simple yet elegant.

She felt his presence before she saw him. Her
head swung nervously and her lashes curled back
from her eyes to reveal the shifting brightness of
the blue iris.

He stood looking at her grimly, head to one side.

'We're the main topic of conversation this morning, I gather,' he said as though they had been talking for hours.

'I'm sorry,' she said.

'For God's sake, stop saying that. You're like a record stuck in a groove.'

She shrugged, making a silent gesture with her hands.

He sat down beside her abruptly. For a moment he said nothing, then he drawled, 'So I leave you cold, do I?'

'Oh,' she muttered, giving him a startled look.

'If you must say things in the canteen expect them to get back to the person concerned within two minutes flat,' he said grimly. 'Especially when the reporter happens to fancy you and is choked because he thinks I might have done better than he has.'

Natalie looked baffled. 'What?'

He made a face. 'You didn't know Tom Leyton fancied you?'

'I've never met him,' she said, wide-eyed.

Jake Lang laughed, but there was no humour in the sound. 'Poor old Tom! He knows you, all right. Would you like to hear what he said about you?'

'No,' she said quickly.

He ignored her. 'He said you were delectable and he'd swop me his train set for you any time.'

She laughed, and then looked surprised because it was a long time since she had laughed with such freedom.

The grey eyes inspected her face intently. 'Why didn't you tell me your husband was dead?'

She was grave immediately, her laughter gone. Meeting his eyes, she said quietly, 'I would have done, but you went before I had a chance.'

He nodded. 'I see. I owe you an apology. I lost my temper. I've always made it a rule never to get tangled with married women and I thought ...'

'You made it clear what you thought,' she said coolly.

'Yes,' he said.

They both stared at the cloudy sky and she shivered. 'I must get back to work.' It was getting cold and the sunshine had all gone. A taxi passing blared its horn and she jumped, glancing round. Her nerves were on edge this morning, she thought.

'You owe me some explanation, though,' he said, rising.

She rose too. 'Explanation?' Then she bit her lip. 'Oh, I see what you mean. I suppose I do.' She walked towards the park exit and he walked beside her, fitting his long strides to her shorter ones, his shoulder beside her own. 'Well, you see....'

'There isn't time now,' he said. 'Have dinner with me.'

'No!' she exclaimed on a horrified note, then softened it quickly. 'It's very kind of you, but no, thank you, I couldn't.'

They came out of the park gates and she saw Sandra and Carol walking a few yards ahead. 'Oh, dear,' she said, staring at their backs.

'What's wrong?'

'Girls from the office,' she said. 'Mr Lang, it really wouldn't do for us to be seen together again. Please, let me go on alone.'

He looked at her thoughtfully, then shrugged. 'Very well.'

'Goodbye,' she said, hurrying after the two girls. When she was in hailing distance of them she slowed, not really wishing to catch them up, then shot a look behind her. Jake Lang was not in view at all. She sighed with relief, then advanced to meet the other two. Carol gave her a quick look.

'Oh, hello. Where did you get to?'

'I had some shopping to do,' Natalie said. Sandra looked pointedly at her empty hands and Natalie gave her a cool glance. 'They hadn't got what I wanted.'

'What was that?' Carol asked, slightly suspiciously.

'Green shoes,' said Natalie. 'To match my dress.'

'I liked the black ones, myself,' said Carol, interested at once and believing her.

Sandra laughed. 'Sure you didn't just happen to bump into Jake Lang?'

Natalie gave her a frosty look. 'Oh, yes, and I met Steve McQueen too, but although he begged me for a date I had to turn him down because tonight I'm going out with Robert Redford.'

'Funny!' Sandra turned her nose up into the air, but Carol gave a grin at Natalie, winking. Sandra had not finished with her yet, though. 'What's he like?' she asked, those pale little eyes avid.

'Robert Redford?' asked Natalie innocently. 'Oh, terribly shy under all that machismo, but I'm working on it.'

'You think you're so clever,' Sandra muttered, walking off fast.

Carol crowed, 'Oh, I enjoyed that! She's a little cat when she's in the mood.'

'When she's on the prowl, you mean,' Natalie said bitterly.

Carol giggled. They had arrived at the enormous office entrance and as they walked through the swing doors a pleasant-looking young man in a fluffy blue

sweater and a pair of dark green jeans arrived behind them. Glancing back, Natalie caught his intent brown stare and wondered why he was gazing
at her in that way. She vaguely felt she had seen him
around, but they had never been introduced.

In the lift he stood beside her, his eyes never moving from her profile. Crossly she glanced round at
last, frowning.

At once he smiled, a very pleasant smile which
she did not have the heart to freeze with a glare.

'Hallo,' he said. 'I thought you'd never notice
me.'

'Who could help it?' she asked coolly. 'Do you
always stare at people like that?'

'Only when they look like you,' he said, and
Carol smothered a spurt of laughter.

Natalie lifted one pale curved eyebrow. 'Is that
this year's top line? It will never take on.'

He grinned in recognition of the snub but said,
'I'm Tom Leyton. I work in the news room and I
love Chinese food.'

'I hate it,' said Natalie as the lift stopped at her
floor. She and Carol walked out and Tom Leyton
came with them. She glanced at him unsmilingly.
'The newsroom is on the floor above,' she pointed
out.

'How about Greek food?' he asked. 'Or French?'

'My culinary tastes are none of your concern,' she
said. 'Goodbye, Mr Leyton.'

'Heartless,' he mourned at her back. 'Beautiful
but heartless. I hoped I had a chance after you said
Jake Lang left you cold.'

She felt her skin run with fire. Of course—that
was where she had heard his name. Jake Lang had
mentioned him. She did not look round, walking

calmly into her office, and Carol scuttled after her with a broad grin.

'Can I tell the office about this one?' she asked plaintively. 'Or is that pass top secret too?'

'Tell who you like,' Natalie said with an impatient sigh. 'What are you, Carol? The office radio?'

'You beast,' Carol retorted, biting her lip, but nevertheless by three o'clock when they broke for tea in the canteen somehow Carol had managed to convey the little story to everyone within earshot, and Natalie heard whispered comment as she sat drinking her tea.

'It's really incredible,' she said to Carol with a frown. 'I've been here for nine months without causing a ripple and I let you talk me into one party only to find myself in the middle of a storm of gossip. Just never ask me to one of your parties again!'

Carol looked subdued, her brown eyes contrite. After a moment she said, 'Still, you look and sound much better than you have done since you arrived, Natalie.'

Natalie was astonished. She stared at her in disbelief. Could it be true? Then she felt a qualm of pain as it suddenly occurred to her that for the first time in a year she had only had Angus very occasionally on her mind. He had become an invisible part of her, haunting her thoughts endlessly, so that she found herself slipping into memory whenever she was alone and often when she was in company. Today he had been largely absent from her thoughts. She had been irritated, disturbed, angry at various times, but she had not been sad.

It was a thought which did not please her. She sat down and began to work again later with thoughtful eyes. As she typed she found herself falling under the mesmeric spell of that deep voice again, so intent on what she was doing that Mrs Dawkins had to lift her headphone and speak loudly to her. 'Mr Lang wants you, Mrs Buchan!'

Natalie started, knowing she had flushed and unable to halt the hot flow of colour. Mrs Dawkins had heard the gossip now, she knew it by her curious stare. As Natalie rose everyone turned to look at her and she stammered to Mrs Dawkins, 'Where? I mean, where do I find him?'

'His office,' said Mrs Dawkins.

'Where is it?'

Mrs Dawkins obviously did not believe in Natalie's ignorance. 'On the fifth floor,' she said after a moment. 'Room 575.'

Natalie had never been to the fifth floor. She stepped out of the lift and stared up and down the corridor. A couple of girls passed her and stared, exchanging looks. Good heavens, she thought, surely the rumours haven't reached up here already? What do they use? Jungle drums?

She tapped on the door and his voice called, 'Come in.'

She would know that voice anywhere now. It was as familiar as her own, strangely individual, with a warm strong timbre which held both charm and assurance.

She went into the room and he sat behind a crowded desk, his elbow on a large book, a cup of tea in his hand. Sipping, he looked at her over the rim of the cup. 'Ah, Mrs Buchan. The tapes,' he said, pointing to the pile of tapes on one corner of the desk.

'Have you finished with them?' she asked, moving to pick them up.

'Sit down for a moment,' he said. 'I want to speak to you.'

'I've got to get back,' she murmured, the tapes in her hands.

'Sit!' he barked, and she was so surprised she obeyed, her lap full of tapes as her hands lowered.

'Put those things down,' he commanded, finishing his tea.

She placed them carefully on the desk and looked at him. 'Well, Mr Lang?'

'Natalie,' he said as if trying out the name. 'It suits you. It could have been tailor-made for you. And if you call me Mr Lang once more I shall strangle you with that beautiful black hair. My name is Jake.'

'I prefer to keep things impersonal between us,' she said in a consciously prim voice.

He laughed, lying back in his chair and swivelling it with one foot.

'My God, how personal do things have to get before you use my name?' The grey eyes taunted her mockingly. 'Or have you conveniently forgotten that only last night you let me take your clothes off?'

She jumped out of the chair and dashed towards the door, but he got there first and his arm barred her way. 'Oh, no,' he said softly. 'You don't run out on me like that. You agreed you owe me an explanation and I want it now.'

Natalie stood here, head bent, hands curled at her side. 'I've already apologised. I was a little drunk last night.'

'Not that drunk,' he said scathingly.

She backed and he pushed her backwards into her chair again. Standing over her, he watched her lowered eyes and flushed cheeks. Then he sat down on the edge of the desk, his foot swinging just within the angle of her vision.

'Now tell me why you threw yourself at me last night,' he said.

'I didn't!' There was shame in her voice.

'We both know you did. I felt someone watching me at that party and when I looked around there you were, staring at me as though you'd been pole-axed. Why?'

She sighed. 'You look like my husband,' she said.

He was silent, the swinging foot still. 'How like?'

'Not very,' she muttered. 'Only from the back, the shape of your head, your hair, your build. When I saw your face I realised....'

'But you saw my face for quite a while before we got to your flat,' he said in a clipped voice.

She covered her face with her hands. 'Please,' she said through her fingers. 'I can't talk about it any more.'

'You're going to have to,' Jake said curtly. 'I want to hear the whole truth. Once we were at your flat why did you let me go on?'

'I don't know,' she whispered shakily, still hiding behind her hands.

He pulled them down forcibly, hurting. His hand pushed her chin up and her anguished eyes met his.

'Pretending, were you?'

She shifted her eyes, finding it very hard to look at him. 'Yes,' she breathed huskily.

'Thanks,' he muttered. 'That does my ego a hell of a lot of good.'

She opened her mouth to speak and he broke in before she could utter a word.

'Say you're sorry again and I swear I'll hit you!'

Natalie closed her mouth. 'What can I say?' she asked after a pause. 'You see, yesterday was my wedding anniversary.'

'Oh, God,' he muttered, moving away.

He stood with his back to her, staring out of the window, his hands in his pockets. 'Go on,' he said after a moment or two. 'How long is it since he died?'

'Just over a year. We were driving to see his parents in Scotland. A lorry jackknifed across the road in front of us. Angus tried to brake, but the car skidded and. . . .' She broke off, breathing thickly, the terrible pain in her chest again. She had dreamt of it night after night. 'When I came out of the anaesthetic I asked the nurse about him and she said he was all right. They didn't tell me for days.'

'Were you married long?'

She laughed miserably without amusement. 'It wasn't even a year. That's why we were going to Scotland, to celebrate the anniversary with his family—we planned to do it alternate years. The first with his parents, the second with mine.'

'And this is the second?'

'Yes,' she said. 'Then yesterday I lost my wedding ring.'

He made a sound of rough disbelief.

'Oh, I found it again, but not until this morning. Yesterday I was so upset about that. I cried and Carol . . . she's a friend of mine . . . she made me go to that party. To cheer me up, she said. I didn't want to go, I didn't want to go at all. There wasn't much to eat and I was almost empty, but they kept filling my glass and I knew I was feeling light-headed. I was going when I saw you.'

She was silent and he said nothing either, his back to her. Then he said grindingly, 'Why did he have to look like me?'

There was no answer to that. Natalie stood up and picked up the tapes. 'I know you're tired of hearing it, but I am sorry, Mr Lang.' She went out quietly and he just stood there without turning round or saying a word.

CHAPTER THREE

SHE hoped that the rumours would be scotched by her care never to be seen with Jake Lang again, but Sandra refused to allow the story to die. Natalie was well aware who was at the bottom of it. Whenever she passed a little knot of girls they fell silent and she saw them look at her curiously, smiling. Often Sandra was among them and her pale blue eyes had a malicious, envious gleam whenever she looked at Natalie. The nine months during which she had worked among them so inconspicuously were over. Her quiet, cool manner seemed to them now a cloak for something else, and they felt she had pulled the wool over their eyes. Their feelings were not eased by another result of that disastrous party: the men in the building now saw Natalie in a new way, too.

Tom Leyton was only the first to make a pass at her. Others soon showed an interest, too. She found herself fending them off in the most unexpected places. Walking through a corridor, in the lift, eating her sandwiches in the park, she was asked for dates by men she barely remembered meeting.

Someone less retiring might have been flattered, swept off her feet. Natalie was half irritated, half alarmed. She did not want all this attention. She had never enjoyed masculine advances, they caused in her an immediate desire to retreat hastily. Her shyness had largely been hidden long ago under a calm exterior, but it was still present in her nature. She was a one-man woman—Angus had been her world. In most respects, he still was, and she had no desire to alter that.

Jake Lang had changed her outward image at the office, though. The men had noticed her before, of course, but she had too firmly rejected all interest until that night. Now they imagined she was open to suggestion and the only result of her immediate rejections was to convince the whole place that something was going on between her and Jake.

It was when she finally accepted that the gossip was not going to die a rapid death that she panicked and accepted a date with Tom Leyton. He seemed the least troublesome of those who had asked her out. She quite liked him, indeed. He had a smile which brought a returning smile from her. His manner was easy, friendly and kind. He was also persistent, and persistence had its own reward in the end.

Meeting her as she walked to the office one sunny April morning he gave her his quick grin and asked: 'Like the theatre?'

'Very much,' she said, half expecting what was to come.

'I've got tickets for a play tomorrow. One of our staff writers wrote it and a theatre club are putting it on for three nights. Care to see it?'

'Which staff writer?' Natalie asked without much interest.

'Anthea Redmond. Know her?'

Natalie did. Very petite with red-blonde hair, the girl came and went in the script department, her arms jingling with ethnic bracelets which she pushed up and down as she talked. She had a high, quick voice which sounded like the shrill call of some seabird, and she was very demanding where work was concerned. She accepted no excuses, no delays, and scrutinised all work with an eagle eye, far more ruthlessly than any of the men ever did.

'What sort of play is it?' she asked, frowning, trying to imagine the sort of work Anthea Redmond would produce for her own pleasure. The scripts she did for the documentary department were necessarily of a functional nature and her own personal style might be quite different.

Tom Leyton looked eagerly at her, scenting the possibility of an acceptance. 'Progressive,' he said, grimacing. 'Theatre in the round involving the audience—you know the sort of thing. A lot of people from Metropolis will be there, though. It could be fun.'

It was precisely the sort of occasion Natalie was looking for, she realised. If she was seen dating Tom Leyton so publicly the office would have to abandon their belief that she was Jake Lang's property.

'Thank you, I'd like to come,' she said, and saw Tom Leyton's face light up with pleasure.

'Great,' he grinned, and his hand went under her elbow. The little gesture was oddly touching, as though he felt he now dared to claim the right to such an intimacy, small though it was, and she did not withdraw from him.

She did not bother to tell anyone she was going out with Tom. It would be round the office fast enough the moment they were seen together at the play.

However, she had reckoned without Tom Leyton himself. When she went down to coffee at eleven it soon became obvious everyone knew. Beneath the calm mask of her face Natalie was amused and irritated. Carol gave her that neglected look. 'Why didn't you tell me? And how can you? Tom Leyton after Jake Lang? You're mad!'

'I did tell you there was nothing between me and Mr Lang,' Natalie protested, 'but you just refused to believe me. Is that my fault?'

'But Tom Leyton!' Carol groaned.

'What's wrong with him? I like him.'

'Oh, he's nice enough, but he's hardly star material.'

'Has it occurred to you that I may not want star material?'

Carol gazed at her. 'As I said, you're mad. If I'd had a chance at Jake Lang I wouldn't let him go so easily.'

'I told you he left me cold,' Natalie said smoothly, and she said it quite deliberately now, loud enough to be heard. In for a penny, in for a pound, she told herself. She had to kill those rumours at any cost. She was not going to be publicly written down as any man's property, and she owed it to Mr Lang to make sure she got him off the hook. He must be finding it embarrassing to be in such an invidious position. She knew he was angry about what happened between them, and she could imagine it made him angrier to have such stories circulating about them.

It was a shock, therefore, to see him a few tables away as she and Carol left the canteen. Natalie felt herself blush and quickly looked away, the long black hair flowing over her shoulders as she walked. He had worn a cold, expressionless mask as their eyes met briefly, but she already knew him well enough to feel the anger vibrating from him. He had heard what she said.

She worked hard on his tapes, taking extra care with the scripts, chiding herself for doing so yet somehow trying to placate him by turning in her best work. Listening to that voice, transcribing those fluent, clever and spellbinding words made her feel she was beginning to know him very well. Most people worked from a well-prepared script from which they never deviated, but Jake Lang had clearly used merely a basic note on which he built his script as he spoke it, improvising brilliantly, filling in details as they came into his mind. The end result was dazzling, like listening to a man talking to a friend, smooth and warm and confidential. Natalie found parts of it coming into her head when she was alone in her apartment that evening. She sat curled up in her chair, her feet tucked under her like a little girl, thinking about the script. Considering the incredible complexity of the subject he had taken an enormous risk in doing it that way, yet it had come off. A prepared and strictly observed script might have sounded wooden, over-rehearsed. It was not surprising that he had such a high reputation.

Across the room Angus's face watched her from their wedding photograph and she looked at him gently. There had been a stage at which she had talked to him as though he could hear her, but now she merely smiled at the photograph, thinking: What else can I do, darling? I've put the poor man in quite a spot. And after behaving so badly.

The following evening she met Tom Leyton after work for dinner. He had rung her during the day to ask what sort of food she liked and she had told him English, preferably.

Over the meal he talked easily, an entertaining companion who made no demands on one, and Natalie listened without speaking much, smiling.

He asked her no questions about herself, merely skating over personal subjects, but as they left he looked down at her face and said: 'You're a listener, not a talker, aren't you?'

'Am I?' Natalie laughed and his eyes touched on the soft pink mouth with such open admiration that her laughter halted at once and her eyes lowered.

'Don't,' he said, taking her arm as they walked to his car, and she looked at him in puzzled question.

'Don't what?'

'Turn off.'

She opened her eyes wide. 'How do you mean?'

'Don't you know you do it? Just now and then a little glimpse of the real girl flashes out and then the light goes off and everything is dark,' he said quietly.

Natalie was taken aback. What was the real girl? she asked herself. She didn't know. How could he?

The theatre club was housed in a stately Edwardian red brick building with ornate gilded decor and plush seats and curtains. It was small, comfortable and charming inside. Tom had good seats in the stalls from which he pointed out to her various familiar faces, some of which she could put a name to, others she never recalled having seen at all. Tom knew them all and got waves and smiles and interested glances in reply to his distant greetings.

When the lights went down and the chatter of the house muted to a soft anticipatory hush, Natalie settled back in her seat with relief. At least now she could just sit back and watch the unfolding of the play with interest. It was then that she first noticed the deep thrust of the stage which came out over the orchestra pit and reached into the audience. The play began at the back of the theatre, startling her. The voice of the first speaker made her jump and look round. Another voice spoke from a different corner of the audience and she swung round there. After a while she realised just what Tom had meant by progressive theatre. The play came at one from all quarters as though the actors were part of the audience. They spoke to people in the seats, they appeared to be holding a dialogue with the audience, although she noticed that they did not seem too keen on it becoming a dialogue in which the audience took part. When someone retorted the actors looked irritated and ignored him.

The lights came up later and Tom grinned at her. 'Well?'

'Very muddled,' said Natalie. 'I don't see what she's getting at, if anything.'

'Come and have a drink,' he suggested, amused. 'The best part of the play tonight, I'm afraid.'

The semi-circular bar was packed. Tom left her in a corner and fought his way through the press. Natalie leaned against the wall and listened and watched those around her, suppressing a smile at their comments on the play, most of which echoed her own view, although some took it more seriously, insisting that it was 'important' drama.

There was an enormous mirror in the centre of the wall. Natalie moved slightly and inspected her own reflection for signs of wear and tear. She brushed back untidy strands of the long black hair. Really, she must have it styled soon. The creamy tweed suit she wore gave her skin a softer smoothness which pleased her, but the silk tie collar of her shirt had come undone. As she tied it neatly her eyes wandered and in the mirror she met Jake Lang's grey eyes. Her features froze. He was standing on the far side of the bar, a glass of whisky in his hand, watching her reflection without expression. There was a dreamlike unreality about seeing his image imposed beside her own, and she shivered.

Then Tom arrived with their drinks and she gratefully looked at him with a smile far warmer than any she had given him that evening. He looked surprised, then delighted.

'Missed me?' His grin was teasing yet held a slightly more serious thought in it.

'After that first act I need this drink,' she said lightly, her eyes not quite meeting his, and then before she knew it she found herself glancing at the mirror and meeting Jake Lang's eyes again. She was furious with herself even as it happened. There had been no thought of it in her mind. It was as if her eyes acted without order from her brain, seeking out his reflection.

He was still watching her, but as she looked at him he looked away, raising his glass to his lips and swallowing the half glass of whisky at great speed. Perhaps after the first act he, too, had needed a drink. He looked as though he did.

The bell rang violently and everyone swallowed their drinks and by the time the second bell had gone they were on their way back to their seats. As the lights went down that time, Tom found Natalie's hand. For one second she thought of pulling her fingers from his grasp, then she let them stay, remembering her motive for coming out with him.

In the half-darkness as the play proceeded she

found her eyes wandering through the forest of
heads in front of them, apparently idly, yet suddenly she realised she was looking for one head and
her blood ran cold. From the back he could be
Angus, and there was a strange nagging need in her
to look at the well-shaped back of his black head.
It was absurd, despicable, but she could not stop
herself from searching for him.

It was only as she and Tom left the theatre at the
end of the play that she saw Jake Lang again.
Natalie was furious with herself at the peculiar sensation of relief and pleasure she felt as her eyes
caught their first glimpse of him. He stood talking
to someone at the back of the theatre, the hard
assurance of his profile cut in shadow on the wall
behind him.

'There's our author,' said Tom Leyton, seeing the
glance she gave the two people laughing at that
moment. Then he added rather coolly, 'With Jake,
of course,' and flicked a look at her. 'But he leaves
you cold, doesn't he? You wouldn't be interested.'

Just then the high, shrill voice of Anthea Redmond broke in upon them. 'Tom darling!' She held
out her hands with a graceful gesture somehow
marred by the jingle of those bracelets. Did she wear
them even in bed? Natalie thought.

Tom took her hands and kissed her on the cheek.
'Congratulations, Anthea. Fantastic! Super!'

Anthea gave a small laugh, the quick expressive
movements of her tiny hands filled with self-deri-
sion. 'You hated it. Half the audience did. I'm not
blind, Tom sweetie. But if one never tries something new one is stationary.'

'True,' Tom murmured with a droll face.

Anthea pinched his cheek. 'Beast! I don't know why I put up with you.'

'My gorgeous physique?' he suggested modestly.

'Well, it wouldn't be your brain, would it, darling?' Anthea gave him a dry smile, lashes fluttering.

Natalie stood beside Tom without speaking, her slender body somehow graceful even when not in motion, the calm planes of her oval face without expression. She could feel Jake Lang's eyes on her, but she did not glance towards him. Tom's hand moved, searching for hers, and she permitted him to take it. Anthea gave her a quick, shrewd look.

'I've seen you before somewhere. From Metropolis?'

'The script department,' Natalie answered.

'Have you typed for me?'

'Once,'' said Natalie, remembering the occasion well.

Anthea's restless eyes flicked up and down, taking in every detail of her appearance. 'I can't quite place your name, I'm afraid.'

'Natalie Buchan,' Tom said brightly.

And Anthea looked at Jake Lang. There was a curious little silence and Natalie found herself staring at him while he stared back.

Then Anthea took his arm, her thin fingers curled possessively around it, smiling up at him. 'We must hurry, darling, or the party will start without us. Nice to have seen you, Tom. Natalie.' Her glance did not quite include Natalie, however. It stopped at Tom and the exclusion was deliberate.

'Party?' Tom asked plaintively.

Natalie sensed Anthea's irritation, but the other girl smiled at Tom, all the same. 'I'm having a party for the crowd tonight. Didn't I ask you? I'm sure I did. You know my apartment. Come along later.'

'We'd love to,' Tom said cheerfully.

The red-blonde hair was suddenly all they could see of Anthea, but her displeasure was felt. As she and Jake Lang walked away, Natalie said quietly, 'I'm afraid I can't come, Tom. I want to get some sleep tonight. Just drop me and go on to the party, though.'

He tried to persuade her all the way back to her apartment, but she was adamant. When they parked he slid an arm along the back of her seat and bent towards her. She let him kiss her once, then drew away. 'Goodnight, Tom, and thank you. I enjoyed it.'

She was gone before he had a chance to say anything more and she heard him drive away as she let herself into her flat.

In bed later she thought of the moment when she saw Jake Lang in the mirror and wondered at the hidden coils of her subconscious, knowing that when she saw him the rest of the crowd in the bar had suddenly become invisible. She must not let him become an obsession, she thought. She must get a grip on herself.

Her date with Tom had the desired result, however. Carol innocently reported that fact to her. 'Everyone's agog. Imagine dropping Jake for Tom Leyton, but then, as Sandra says: whatever turns you on!'

Natalie had not intended to see Tom again, but she realised that she had to maintain the fiction for a little while, so she accepted two further invitations from him. One evening they had dinner and saw a film. Another time he took her to a pop concert for which he had been given complimentary tickets. Then he was suddenly sent to China to do a report on East–West relations and Natalie lapsed into her previous quiet life without regret. While he was away several of the younger men tried to date her, but they accepted her excuse that 'Tom wouldn't like that!'

She was on the last tape of Jake's series when one evening she opened the door of her apartment to a peremptory ring and found him on the doorstep.

'Oh!' she exclaimed, aghast. She had just washed her hair and it was still damp, hanging round her face in limp coils.

'I want to talk to you,' he said, his face imperturbable. 'May I come in?'

Natalie hesitantly looked down at the blue cotton wrap she wore. 'I'm not dressed for visitors.'

'This is business, not social,' he said.

She stepped back reluctantly and he walked into her apartment, bringing with him so vivid a recollection of his other visit that her whole face burned.

She took him into the little sitting-room and he glanced at the hair dryer she had put down to answer the door bell.

'My hair is still damp,' she said uneasily, not able to meet his eyes.

'Finish drying it, then,' he said. 'I don't want you catching cold because of me.'

'It doesn't matter. What did you want to talk to me about?'

'Dry your hair,' he repeated, walking to the bureau and picking up her wedding photograph.

She sat down and hurriedly began to blow-dry her hair, brushing it as she directed the warm air across it. She could not hear anything much above the hum of the machine, but she watched him staring at the photograph and wondered what he was thinking.

She could read nothing from his face. It was a mask. He put the photograph down and sauntered along the shelf containing her books. Here and there he picked one out, glanced into it, replaced it. He was wearing a dark suit and the formal clothes were preferable to the sexy jeans and shirt he had worn the night they met. He looked withdrawn, a stranger. He stood with his back to her and she stared at that familiar head, her throat going dry. I wish he would go back to Africa, she thought. Am I to be haunted by the back of his head for the rest of my life?

As she switched off the dryer he turned and surveyed her, making her very conscious of her state of undress, the bare legs he could see beneath the wrap, the tiny blue fur mules into which her feet were pushed.

'I've been very impressed by the work you've been doing on my series,' he said coolly.

'Thank you.' That pleased her. She had wanted to impress him.

'You've done a good job. I couldn't fault it.'

Had he tried? she wondered.

'In fact,' he went on slowly, 'you've done such an excellent job that I wondered if I could tempt you to leave the script department and come to work for me.'

Natalie felt a coldness shiver through her blood. 'No,' she said without even stopping to think and her voice was hoarse.

He looked at her and away. His face, his eyes, were quite blank. 'My secretary vanished while I was in Africa and I've been waiting for a replacement, but all the girls I've interviewed have been either brainless or dull. I've spoken to the head of Scripts and he's prepared to let you go.'

She stood up shakily, hands wringing in an attitude of dismay. 'You must realise it's impossible.'

'Why?' His glance was cool and direct.

She felt her face burning again. 'Because....' She could not put it into words.

He raised a dark eyebrow. 'Yes?'

Natalie could have hit him. He knew. Why was he pretending not to? 'It's obvious, Mr Lang.'

'Not to me,' he said coldly.

She stared at him numbly, and he looked back, the casual way he lounged there infuriating. 'I couldn't,' she whispered.

'Am I that irresistible?' he asked, and the derisive gleam of the grey eyes made her angry.

'You know very well what I'm talking about! I've gone to great trouble to stop all that gossip and if I went to work for you it would start up again.'

His eyes narrowed. 'What trouble did you go to?'

They stared at each other and she could not answer.

'Leyton,' he said slowly. 'So that's why you went out with him.'

'Partly,' she said in a quick way. 'I like him, too, but it seemed a good way of cutting off all that talk about....' She stopped dead.

'About us,' he said, and smiled tightly. 'Lucky for you that I don't make confidences to my friends. I may not have finished what I started, but I'm willing to bet I got further than Leyton did.'

'Don't!' she muttered, bending her head. 'I explained.'

'You're too sensitive,' he said curtly. 'Does it matter? Now that I understand the situation I've lost interest anyway, Mrs Buchan. No man wants to be used as a substitute for a dead husband. I don't believe in ghosts and I've no intention of becoming one in your bed.'

She was scarlet, unable to look at him. 'I was drunk. It would never happen again.'

'No,' he agreed harshly. 'I damned well wouldn't let it.'

He pivoted on his heel and picked up the photograph, staring at it. 'I'm damned if I see any resemblance.'

'I told you there was very little facially,' she said huskily. 'Just from the back in a poor light.'

'And I don't intend to stand with my back to you in the dark for ever,' he said drily. He studied the picture in silence for a while. 'Not bad looking, was he?'

She didn't answer. Angus was more than just a well-formed set of features, a smile, a pair of commanding grey eyes. Love saw beneath the surface of a face, but she had no intention of explaining all that to Jake Lang.

Without looking at her, still staring at the photograph, he said quietly, 'Take the job with me. You're intelligent and ambitious, I would say. It's a chance in a million and you know it.'

It was true. Most of the girls in the pool dreamt of a chance like that, an opportunity to get into the programme side of the work, and especially as Jake Lang's secretary. They would swoon at the very suggestion!

'Thank you for asking me, but no,' she said. He

wasn't a fool. He knew her reasons without needing to have them explained.

He put the photograph down and turned to look at her, then, 'I'm going to do some blunt speaking,' he said crisply, pushing his hands into his pockets, the movement displacing his jacket so that the trim-waisted figure was revealed. 'First, gossip will obviously start up again, but you'll have to learn to live with that. There's always talk in a place like Metropolis.'

'Possibly, but I still dislike being the target of gossip,' Natalie exclaimed.

He ignored the interruption, the even tenor of his voice cool. 'Secondly, I promise you there's no reason to fear a repetition of what happened the first time we met.' Her eyes flew to his face, widening. 'I happen to find girls with your particular brand of looks rather attractive, I admit,' he continued in an expressionless fashion which made it sound as though the subject bored him. 'To put it crudely, I fancy you, and I won't deny that you could still make me want you.'

She stared down at the floor, her face going hot.

'You'll notice I said make me,' he went on. 'Because I can give you a categoric assurance that nothing on this earth would get me to touch you, the way you are at the moment.'

She drew breath sharply, and then asked herself why that remark should sting. She did not want him to desire her, yet for some inexplicable reason what he had just said had annoyed her.

'So if you're refusing the job because you're afraid I shall permanently be making passes at you, forget it, because I can promise you I won't. I'm offering you a job because I approve of your work and I'm desperately in need of a secretary I can trust. I may consider you to be misguided, even warped, in your personal life, but I think you would make an excellent secretary.'

Natalie still remained silent, turning over what he had said in her mind and forced to believe him. The very coolness of his voice and face were somehow convincing.

'Do you want to sit in the pool all your working life?' he asked her impatiently. 'I think we could work together. This series is going to take me a year to put together and I like to have the best team I can get. For my money you're the best secretary I'm likely to run across if I look for another year. You have one inestimable quality I haven't mentioned.'

Her curiosity aroused, she asked him, 'What's that?'

'A beautiful lucid silence,' he said drily, his mouth quirking. 'I never remember meeting a woman who spoke less. Yet your face is very expressive. It speaks for you. Frankly, when I'm working the last thing I want is a woman chattering away next to me.'

She could believe that. Since he returned she had heard stories about his working manner. Irritable, sharp and demanding, the girls said—and that was on his good days.

He caught her half smile and looked at her enquiringly. 'What did I say to amuse you, I wonder?'

She shook her head. 'Nothing.'

Jake pushed a hand through the thick black hair and the hard bones of his face tightened as if in anger. 'Well, I've put my side of it. What do you say?'

Natalie sighed. 'I'd have to think about it.'

'Not for too long, then,' he said. 'I have to get someone soon. The office is knee deep in paper.'

She smiled. 'I remember—I did notice.'

He smiled back. 'You see, I really need you.' He walked to the door. 'Let me know your decision as soon as you can, will you?'

Natalie followed, her slender body moving lightly and gracefully in the skimpy wrap which revealed all the sensuous lines of her figure. Jake turned at the door close to her and looked down at her, eyes drifting over her.

'You're very beautiful,' he murmured coolly. 'Beautiful but lifeless, like some wraith. Even those gorgeous blue eyes have no light in them. How old are you?'

'Twenty-four.'

He made a face. 'Too young to bury yourself alive.' He leaned back against the front door, hands in his pockets. 'Was he a passionate lover?'

'Why must you ask questions like that?' she demanded, flushing.

'Because I'm curious about the answers,' he drawled. 'Looking at you now I sometimes think I imagined the passionate woman I held in my arms that night. I thought I'd found the perfect lover. You came into my arms so silently and yet with such hunger....'

'I wish you wouldn't talk about it,' she muttered, biting her lip. 'It's very embarrassing.'

'Is that why you hesitate about the job? Or is it the gossip?'

'A mixture of both,' she said.

'I don't think it's either,' he returned in a cool voice. 'I suspect you can't tolerate the thought that

I know so much about you that you prefer to keep hidden. We found out a lot about each other that night. You wish I would just vanish, don't you?'

'Yes,' she whispered, staring into his eyes.

'I'm sorry,' he said brusquely, 'but I've no intention of doing any such thing. What happened that night is part of you, Natalie, and you have to face that sooner or later. You're trying to live in a vacuum, filling it with dead dreams of a love which has ended.'

'No,' she cried, distraught. 'It isn't over. While I'm alive, Angus is alive.'

'That's true,' he said sombrely. 'But only as the past, your past. He can't inhabit the present or the future. You have to do that, and you have to face up to the reality of his death. Until you do, you'll be half alive yourself, and that would be a crime against life.'

'You don't understand.' Natalie struggled to explain to him, to make him see her feelings, the impossibility of treachery to Angus, the disloyalty and betrayal she felt was involved in caring for anything or anybody else.

She couldn't say any of it. She could only look at him distractedly, her face now as white as it had been red.

'Oh, I understand,' he said coolly. 'Only too well. You've got to break out of that vacuum before it turns your warm human blood to ice water and leaves you as dead as your husband.'

'You're cruel,' she said faintly, shivering at the description.

His mouth twisted and there was cruelty in the lines of it. 'Perhaps it's time someone was cruel to you,' he shrugged, and she almost felt he enjoyed the thought of that. 'Perhaps what you need is a little cruelty.'

'I think you'd enjoy it,' she said accusingly. 'I dented your ego when I admitted you reminded me of Angus, didn't I? I remember, you said as much. You aren't used to being second-best. You expect women to fall over in a swoon if you so much as look at them. You're not a very likeable man, Mr Lang.'

His eyes glittered angrily. 'Maybe not, but I'm alive.' He pulled open the door, looking back at her. 'And yes, Mrs Buchan, I'd enjoy being cruel to you. I'd get great enjoyment from it and I don't give a damn whether you find me likeable or not. You deserve to be treated with cruelty. You haven't got the courage of a mouse. Stay huddled inside your safe little mousehole for the rest of your life, but one day you're going to wake up and find it's too late for you to start living, and I doubt if the ghost of a dead man will help you then, Mrs Buchan.'

He had gone, the door rattling after him. Natalie stood in the hall and stared at the shivering door panels. He had really lost his temper, she thought, half dazedly. There had been a white-hot rage in his face. Masculine aggression always did make her feel nervous and she was shaking now as though he had actually hit her.

The cruel things he had said hit her in shock wave after shock wave. Was she a coward? She had never thought herself one. Angus was dead and she was alive. It hurt. She put her arms around her waist, bending, a groan issuing deeply from her stomach. Some of what he said had been said to her before. Angela had said some of it, less harshly, but with the same intention, she thought.

Angela always spoke the truth as she saw it. Natalie straightened with a pale face. She would ask Angela for her opinion. She respected her sister's intelligence. Angela would help her make up her mind about whether or not to take this job.

At the weekend she sat in Angela's garden while the children sang and shouted as they played around them on the lawn and outlined the whole story, carefully toning down exactly what had happened that night between her and Jake Lang.

Although she left that part veiled Angela's eyes had a curious, comprehending gleam in them as she looked at her. 'Attractive, is he?'

'Very,' Natalie said rather coldly.

'Take the job,' said Angela. She looked round and screamed, 'Tony, don't eat that worm!'

'Why not?' Tony asked. 'Birds eat worms.'

'Are you a bird?' Angela asked unanswerably.

Tony, however, always answered questions, however rhetorical. He had a logical mind. 'No,' he agreed. 'I haven't got no wings.'

'Then don't eat worms. Put it back in the flower bed.'

'I want to watch it wriggle first,' he said, releasing the worm and bending over it.

Angela looked back at Natalie. 'Take the job,' she said again. 'You must be mad to hesitate. As he said, it's a chance in a million. He sounds as if he's got his head screwed on. I've told you what I think before—it's time you stopped living in the past. You had a bad stroke of luck, but forget it now and get on with living. Angus would say the same, you know he would.'

Natalie did know. Angus had always been direct,

confident and aggressive towards life. She sat in the garden with the spring sunshine giving her creamy skin a warm blush and listened to the sweet singing of a thrush on a songpost in another garden. The sun's warmth made her body warmly relaxed. I'm alive, she thought. Angela is right, I've got to make the effort. What had Jake Lang said? That the way she was behaving was a crime against life itself? The words had made a deep impression on her. They came back now, haunting her. She thought of that hard, cruel mouth as he spoke coldly and angrily to her. He was nothing like Angus. Why had she ever thought he was? There would be no danger in working with him. He left her cold.

CHAPTER FOUR

A MONTH later, Natalie answered the telephone in Jake Lang's office, her voice abstracted, a faint frown on her brow. 'Yes? Mr Lang's secretary speaking.'

'So he leaves you cold, does he?' asked an accusing voice, and she sat up, her abstraction falling away.

'Tom? You're back, then?'

'Oh, I'm back,' he said in a voice filled with hostility. 'And to what? The minute I walked in the building I got it from all sides. They couldn't wait to tell me. Natalie, you've disillusioned me.'

She smiled, hearing the slight undertone of make-believe in his voice. Tom was not as angry as he was pretending. A little piqued, maybe, but not deeply wounded, just playing at it.

'Did you have a nice trip?' she asked.

'Do you care?'

'I'd be sorry to hear you'd been eaten by a panda at Peking Zoo,' she protested.

He laughed. 'You little beast! You remind me of a fairy story my sister used to love.'

'Really? You must tell it to me some time, but I've heard quite a few fairy stories, I'm afraid, Tom. I might get bored.'

He laughed again. 'I'm damned sure I wouldn't. At the risk of boring you, will you have dinner with me?'

'Tonight? I'd love to, but I'm working until seven-thirty. We've a tape session booked at six.'

'Jake working you hard?'

'Like a slavemaster,' she agreed. But it was exhilarating to work for someone as certain of himself as Jake Lang. It was exciting learning the business of programme editing close at hand. Working in the script department had been fine, but this was the real thing. They were actually making something. Natalie could watch the programme emerging from the rough-hewn mould as Jake delicately planed and sliced it.

'I'll pick you up dead on seven-thirty,' Tom said flatly. 'And if Jake tries to stop us leaving I'll flatten him.'

Amusement touched her face, altering the smooth cool mask of it between the flowing dark hair. 'I'll tell him,' she said, tongue in cheek, and rang off.

She had been working for Jake Lang for three weeks now. The news of her promotion had hit the script department like a giant wave and some of the girls had drowned in envious dismay. Sandra had been vicious in her comment, not even bothering to make her remarks out of Natalie's hearing.

'Now we know why you snatched him at that party, don't we? Cool as a cucumber to all the other men, then you flip over Jake Lang inside five minutes. Clever stuff! We should have guessed there was something behind your innocent face. The grieving widow act had us all fooled, though.'

Natalie had winced at the brutality of that last remark. Lifting her head defiantly, she had shrugged. 'Whatever I said, you'd read your own interpretation into Mr Lang offering me the job.'

'You bet I would,' Sandra muttered, pale blue

eyes spiteful. 'From what I know of Jake Lang I can guess the incentive you gave him to get that job. He doesn't do anything for nothing. Everyone knows he's tough, ambitious and ruthless. How do you think he's got where he is today? The world is littered with the people he stamped on to get to the top.'

Natalie had shivered, half believing her, remembering the cold, angry eyes with which he had surveyed her before he slammed out of her flat. Ruthless. Oh, yes, she thought, he's undoubtedly that. But then what else would he be? The weak don't climb ladders, they form them. Jake Lang was one of the strong who shoot to the top whatever they have to do to get there. She knew all about men like that. Angus had been one—oh, not callous or cold, but powerful. One knew that just watching the way he played rugger. He played to win and, although she had never seen him stamp on anybody to get his own way, she had seen him shove them out of his path with a hand planted in their face to knock them away. She had seen him bring a large, muscled player down with a flying tackle and then get away with the ball before the other could crawl to his knees.

Of course, Jake Lang was not Angus, yet she suspected he would play with the same ferocity and determination to win.

She was sitting at her desk with her head propped in her hands, gazing at the blue sky beyond the window. It was odd, she thought, that she should be attracted to men whose nature was so alien to her own.

'Have you got that file?'

She jumped at the crisp demand and turned, still

deep in thought, her blue eyes dreamy.

Jake stared, eyes narrowing. 'Snap out of it! You're here to work, not daydream. I won't have my office haunted by ghosts, either.'

Colour ran up her skin and her eyes took on a dark blue anger. 'I put the file on your desk,' she retorted, chin high.

He walked round the desk and picked up the file, flicking over it with a bent head. She watched him angrily and he looked up, the grey eyes icy. 'Get on with your work.'

Lips compressed to stop a retort escaping, she obeyed, and after a moment he walked out again, closing the door so quietly that she would have preferred him to bang it. She had already discovered that Jake's rage was easier to bear when he was violent than when he was quiet. She had always disliked explosions of wrath, but she found she disliked even more a man who became ice-hot with it, his eyes glittering coldly in a taut face. In those moods he used words like knives and they could rend the flesh. She had seen a studio controller burst into tears and run weeping off the floor when he used that voice on her. Even the men looked wary and avoided him in those moods. Luckily, they came infrequently, but when they did everyone was as careful as a cat walking on eggshells.

He had no sense of time. When he was working he concentrated with all his attention on what he was doing, and woe betide anyone who tried to break off before Jake indicated that they could. In private some of his colleagues bewailed his refusal to take their private lives into account. Wives detested the sound of his name, Natalie gathered. It was no excuse for a tape editor to plead a wedding anniversary or a wife's birthday. Jake looked at them scathingly and with open contempt. 'It can wait.'

At times they seemed to be his favourite words. People mimed them behind his back when one of the others stammered a request to leave early. 'A date?' Jake would ask, mouth acid. 'It can wait.' And the others grinned wryly as they mouthed the words with him.

Liam Brown, who did the graphics for the series, came into the office later that afternoon and perched on Natalie's desk, talking to her about a folder of possible ideas he had brought in for Jake's attention. While he talked his hands were busy sketching her. She had grown used to Liam's habit of drawing everything he saw. His thin, long fingers flew across his pad, his liquid dark eyes moving from her to the face emerging under his hand, and all the time he talked, making her wonder how he contrived to do both at once.

'Doing anything tonight?' he asked suddenly, moving his head back to get the sketch into perspective.

Jake walked in at that moment and she tensed, aware of him at once, and aware, too, that he had heard Liam's question. She glanced round and met the steely glitter of his eyes, saw the sharp twist of his mouth. He expected her to refuse to answer, she guessed.

'I've got a date,' she said coolly, looking back at Liam.

'Oh?' Liam looked at Jake and she knew he thought he knew who her date was with; his thin face was expressive, wry.

'Who gave you the right to take up residence on

Mrs Buchan's desk?' Jake enquired in a freezing voice.

Silently Liam slipped down. He detached the sheet on which he had drawn her and handed it to Jake. 'Your property,' he said, and there was a faint dryness in his tone as he walked out of the door.

Jake looked down at it with an expression which almost seemed to hold savagery. Natalie had an odd suspicion that he was going to rip it to pieces.

Instead he walked to the wastepaper basket and dropped it into it. She looked down at the letter she was typing. The words swam before her eyes. Bastard, she thought. I hate him!

'What did he want?' Jake asked curtly. 'Apart from a date with you.'

'Ideas for the graphics,' she said, indicating the folder without looking away from the pad she was working from. She began to type, head tilted to one side so that she could see the copy.

Jake picked up Liam's folder and she heard him turning the sheets. 'Who are you dating?' he asked, and for a second or two she imagined she had heard wrongly, then she said quietly, 'Tom.'

'Ah, yes, I heard he was back.' He walked to his own desk and put the folder down on the cluttered surface. 'Have you been clearing this again? I can't find a damned thing when you've been messing about with my papers.'

'What did you want?' She stopped typing and glanced at him.

'A letter from Daniel Masters.'

'In the files,' she said, getting up. Jake leaned on his desk, watching her walk across the office. She found the letter and took it to him. As she turned to go back to her desk he caught her wrist.

'I thought you only went out with Leyton to stop the gossip about us.'

Natalie looked pointedly at her wrist. 'It hasn't stopped, though, has it?'

'Is that why you're going out with him?'

She tried to pull her wrist out of his grip, but he refused to release it, tightening his fingers so that she gasped and glared at him.

'Answer me,' he ground between his teeth.

'No,' she said, eyes brilliant. 'I like him.'

His hand released her and she rubbed her wrist, seeing the dark red line of his mark with anger.

'Do you have to be such a brute?'

He laughed, but there was no laughter in the grey eyes. They were all ice. 'It gets results.'

'Not with me.'

'Oh, yes,' he said, watching her, his lids half lowered, a strange cold gleam in his eyes. 'With you there's no other way.'

The telephone rang again and he watched her answer it. She spoke coolly, then looked at him without expression. 'Miss Redmond.'

He took the phone and sat down in his chair, swivelling while he talked, his eyes on his shoe. Natalie sat behind her own desk, fingers poised to begin work again, and Jake shot her a hard look, shaking his head. She waited, irritated to have to listen to the intimate, teasing conversation. Anthea Redmond was a frequent caller, a frequent visitor. Jake flirted with her lightly and Natalie knew he was seeing her out of working hours. How close their relationship was, she had no idea. Nor, she told herself, did she care.

As he put down the phone she began to type at once while Jake inspected Liam's folder at his leisure, his feet on the desk, his head tilted back against the back of his chair.

So far, she had to admit, she had found it more fascinating and spellbinding to work with him than she had imagined. Difficult he might be, downright impossible at times, but she was never bored. And he had kept his word. He had never made a single pass. His manner to her, if anything, was hostile, always withdrawn, even unpleasant now and then. She found it easier to cope with than the flattering compliments the others dropped whenever they got the chance to be alone with her.

Angus had once told her that her combination of looks and shyness was a challenge to the men she met. It had taken him weeks to crack the ice of her withdrawal. Her happiness with him had not changed her basic personality. She had remained the same shy, quiet girl he had met, and after his death she had removed even further behind a shielding mask.

Working with Jake Lang had changed her a little, however. For one thing, she was so busy and involved that she had no time to brood about Angus. She worked from eleven to seven every day. By the time she got back to her apartment she was too worn out to do much but take a bath, have a meal and watch television for an hour before crawling off to bed and sleeping like the dead.

At weekends Angela commented on the alteration. 'You're looking better—more colour. Eat that steak, I got it especially for you. And don't hide any of it behind the lettuce. You're not Tony.'

'I'm Tony,' her nephew had pointed out in his logical way. 'I'm four. How old are you, Auntie Nat?'

'Twenty-four,' she had replied, smiling at him, wanting to kiss his freckled snub nose and knowing he would be offended if she did.

'Then you're older than Daddy,' Tony had said, astonished. ' 'Cos he's twenty-one. He told me so.'

Adrian grimaced at his reproving wife. 'He takes things so literally.'

'So don't tell him fairy stories,' Angela retorted.

And that reminded Natalie now of Tom Leyton's remark that she reminded him of a fairy story. When he picked her up at the office later that evening she gave him a curious look and asked him what he had meant.

'The heartless princess,' he explained cheerfully. 'Do you know it?'

'No. What happened to her?'

'She got kissed,' he said, and proceeded to demonstrate before she had a chance to evade him. He kissed very pleasantly and it didn't do a thing to her, but she stood there, making no attempt to get away, because in the middle of it she felt the door open silently and knew Jake stood there watching them.

Tom moved away, inspecting her flushed face with interest. Before he could say anything Jake walked right through the middle of them and Tom looked startled. 'Oh, hi, Jake. Didn't see you.'

'Don't use my office for your necking parties,' Jake snapped, sinking into his chair. His dark brows had a harsh frown between them and his voice was acid.

'Coming, Tom?' Natalie asked, and Tom followed her out of the room. In the lift he glanced at her curiously. 'Was that jealousy or sheer bad temper?'

'The latter,' she said coolly. 'It's his usual condition.'

Tom grinned. 'So I'd heard. Hell on two legs, they say. I've never worked with him, but I've seen the cripples who have and my heart bled for them. Are you sure you're in the right job? A sweet, gentle girl like you could take quite a beating from Jake Lang.'

Natalie shrugged. 'I can cope.'

He eyed her thoughtfully. 'I guess you probably can, at that. Not much throws you, does it?'

Some things did, she thought, and Jake Lang was one of them, but she would die rather than betray that.

The evening with Tom was an unqualified success. He made a very entertaining and pleasant companion. She did not need to make an effort with him. He talked enough for two and he was funny. She found herself laughing often and enjoyed listening to him. When he drove her back to her flat she smiled a goodnight, but before she could go he took her hand and held it between both his, looking hard at her. 'Am I going to see you again?'

'I imagine so, as we both work in the same building.'

He grimaced at her light tone. 'You know what I mean. You're a very evasive girl. I don't know where I am with you. Are you going to let me take you out again soon?'

'If you want to,' she said without particular emphasis, her eyes on his face.

'But no strings?' he said, filling in the unspoken rider.

Natalie shook her head, her black hair sweeping

across her shoulders. 'Definitely no strings, Tom. Friends, that's all.'

'May I ask the reason?' He watched her face closely. 'Have I a rival? Jake Lang, for instance? Or are you just not interested in a closer relationship with anyone than friendship?'

She nodded. 'The latter.'

He looked down at her hand, fingered the wedding ring on it. 'He must have been quite a guy.'

Tears pricked her eyes. 'Yes, he was.'

'I'm sorry.'

She shrugged. 'I'm trying to grow out of self-pity, so don't encourage me, Tom.'

His glance was sharp. 'Who said you were self-pitying?'

'Several people. My sister, for one. And she's right, I know she is, even though I was angry with her at the time.'

'I know a quick cure,' he murmured, smiling.

It was ten minutes before she left the car and Tom had a satisfied look as he snatched a final kiss, but Natalie, although she had not found his kisses unenjoyable, knew he had scarcely swept her off her feet. The fiery hunger which Jake Lang had found so easy to arouse in her had not been awoken by Tom Leyton's lovemaking. She liked him—*but*. And in that one little word lay a continent of feeling.

Lying in her bed later she grimaced. Was it so surprising? After a man like Angus could she seriously expect that a pleasant young man like Tom could light any fires in her?

But there would never be anyone like Angus. Never, she thought. A bleak cold word. She did not relish the prospect of settling for a half-hearted second best love, and if she did accept it, would any man want it?

Jake's reaction had been sufficient warning to her on that point. She felt herself colouring at the memory. The events of the night they met still had the power to make her want to curl up and die of shame.

When he had realised that she had been pretending, as he made love to her, that he was her dead husband, he had been coldly, violently angry. And she could not blame him. Thinking about it objectively she was horrified with the way she had behaved. As Jake had said, no man likes being used as a substitute for another lover. Working with him, she had been taught indelibly that Jake Lang demanded and got nothing less than total commitment. He was icily scathing about anyone who turned in less than their best, expecting dedication to the work, and she was sure that he would apply the same high standards in a love affair.

His ego was powerful. He would never forgive anyone who dented it, as she had.

Next morning she sat, cool and contained, in her chair while he dictated to her, striding around the office. Even though the material he was working on was abstruse and technical, Natalie was conscious of something else on his mind. He was angry; she felt it in the way his eyes knifed her in the back as he walked behind her.

'Get that typed up at once,' he ended curtly, standing beside her, his long hands thrust into his pockets.

'Yes, Mr Lang,' she said quietly, head bent. She found that in his more antagonistic moods it was safest to bend before the storm. Any sort of defiant reaction merely provoked him.

'Enjoyed your date, did you?' he asked with a barbed sharpness in his voice.

'Very much,' she said, sliding paper into her machine.

'I guessed as much,' he muttered, mouth twisting. 'You've been humming some revolting love song under your breath ever since your arrival.'

That surprised her. She hadn't been aware of it, but now she realised he was right. The tune had been on the radio while she was eating her toast for breakfast and it had stuck in her head, as is often the way with casually heard popular music.

Jake stood watching her, the sunlight picking out blue-black lights in his hair, turning them to the iridescent brilliance of a blackbird's wing. Glancing up, Natalie caught that sheen, surprised by her own pleasure in the sight of it into gasping, her mouth parting involuntarily, and Jake's eyes hardened at that look. He bent suddenly and caught her mouth with his own hotly.

It was over too fast for her to react. He straightened, his face mocking. 'Just a small sample for the sake of comparison,' he told her coolly. 'I wouldn't want you to drift into marrying Tom Leyton just because you haven't the nerve to consider the other possibilities.'

Flushed, she asked him, 'What possibilities?' The hard demand of his mouth still burned on her lips. She wanted to touch her own mouth out of sheer curiosity to see if the imprint of Jake's kiss really did show on it, as she somehow felt it must.

His eyes narrowed. 'There are other men in the world. I can think of half a dozen not far from the office who would jump at the chance to take you out.'

Irrationally the reply disappointed her, and that in turn made her irritated. 'I like Tom,' she said flatly.

'Of course you do,' Jake drawled. 'Safe, isn't he? A tame young man who won't hurt you or drag you kicking and screaming out of your dream world into the real one. Of course you like him. But does he know he's a stand-in for a dead man?'

Her eyes flashed. 'He isn't!'

'No?' The cool question was sardonic.

'No,' she denied angrily. 'Tom is different from Angus. I could never confuse the two of them.'

Jake straightened, staring at her, and she received a peculiar impression of menace, cold silent menace. The grey eyes were silvery like cooling iron. The strong mouth was set in a straight, cold line.

She shrank in her chair, puzzled and alarmed. He took a step towards her and she saw cruelty in every line of his face.

Then the door opened and Anthea Redmond swept into the office, jangling like a fire engine. She stopped dead, staring at them and Natalie knew that the other girl had smelt the tension in the room. There was swift, jealous suspicion in her face as she looked at Jake.

He turned, dragging a politely smiling mask down over the unleashed barbarism of his face. 'Well, well, what brings you here?' He looked her up and down, smiling, his mouth slightly crooked. 'That's new. Very daring.'

It was, Natalie thought, giving the orange dress a quick all-seeing glance. The colour gave Anthea a slightly overpowering vibrancy which, coupled with her vivid hair, reminded Natalie of a nasturtium. Anthea smiled, well satisfied with Jake's admiration, and he bent his head to kiss her. Natalie began to type, concentrating on her work, but the image remained imprinted on her mind's eye. Anthea even clung like a climbing nasturtium, she thought viciously, and she hoped those thin little arms would choke Jake as they wound around his neck. Serve him right!

She typed vigorously, barely seeing the words she was transcribing, and beside her the kiss seemed to go on and on. Was Anthea eating him? She shot them a sideways glance out of the corner of her eye. The two of them were entwined as closely as ever.

'Wow!' Anthea purred as Jake at last released her. 'How am I going to work after that?'

'Force yourself,' Jake mocked lightly.

He walked to the door, talking in a low voice, and then Anthea had gone and Jake came back to his own desk and flung himself into the chair, picking up a pile of papers. Natalie was aware of his brief glance and ignored it.

An angry word slipped out of her as she suddenly realised she had missed several lines of the script. She ripped the page from the machine, crumpled it and flung it into her wastepaper basket.

As she wound a fresh sheet into the machine Jake watched, a funny little smile on his mouth.

'Something bothering you?' he enquired.

Fingers poised over the keys she gave him a cool smile. 'Not at all,' she replied calmly. 'I'd missed a line, that's all.'

His mocking expression indicated that he did not believe a word of it, but he said nothing. They both concentrated on their work for the rest of the day, but Natalie was aware of some strange shift in her feelings, a new tension whenever Jake came anywhere near her.

In the weeks that followed she began to find her job increasingly demanding, increasingly exciting. Jake was the core of the whole operation. The team working on the programmes came in and out all the time and since Jake was often absent it was upon Natalie that the whole burden of the daily routine fell. She found she was required to be a walking encyclopaedia on everything concerned with the series. She was constantly asked for her opinion, given questions to which the answers were urgently needed, and as Jake always said impatiently, 'Well, find out,' she found herself doing just that. The more responsibility Jake threw at her, the more she liked her job. Working in the script department she had been a cog in a large, well-oiled machine. Now she was the hub around which the great wheel revolved and although it was tiring she loved it.

She continued to date Tom at irregular intervals, grateful for the excuse her job offered her to turn down too many invitations for Tom to get the wrong idea about their relationship. He sighed and accepted her excuses, knowing perfectly well that work in Jake's department meant a full-time dedication which left little energy for a private life. It was one of the things which made people hesitate about accepting a job with Jake Lang. He was too single-minded to consider their private lives.

One week, indeed, she found herself working from ten in the morning until eight in the evening every day, with a bare hour for lunch, and some of the team worked even longer hours. Their groans of complaint were muttered in her ear since they dared not complain to Jake.

'He's a ruthless devil,' Liam told her. 'One day I'll swing for him, I'm sure of it. What private life do any of us get?' He gave her a curious grin. 'What private life do you get?'

'I manage,' she said lightly, but when he had gone she sat at her desk feeling like something that has been washed up on a beach. She was so tired she could have slept at her desk.

That afternoon while she and Jake worked in their usual silence, Tom wandered into the room and got the full benefit of Jake's most vicious look. A hunted, nervous smile crossed Tom's face.

'Er—hallo,' he said, then looked at Natalie. 'I've got tickets for the ballet. I had to fight six men to get them. You'll come, won't you?'

'When?' she asked him, ignoring the sinister drum of Jake's finger tips on his desk.

'Tonight,' he said.

'She's working,' Jake interrupted. 'We do work here, unlike the news room. Get back there, Leyton, and justify the salary you earn.'

Natalie was furious enough to defy him. Smiling very warmly at Tom, she said, 'I'd love to come, Tom. Pick me up here at seven.'

Beaming, he shot off and Jake leaned over his desk and said bitingly, 'You're working until nine. I want this finished tonight.'

'Do it yourself, then,' she said very sweetly. He almost burst into flames, his eyes leaping, but when Tom arrived Natalie calmly swept out.

CHAPTER FIVE

THE following Friday Jake casually informed her that she would be required to work the next morning. 'It's Saturday,' Natalie answered, staring at him.

'I'm aware of it.' His voice had a dry note in it and the grey eyes were sardonic. 'I'll have to work too. It was the only free time I could get in the audio room—Bookings were digging their heels in over it. Sorry if it interferes with your plans.'

He did not look sorry. He looked as though he didn't give a damn, and that was typical, she thought.

'Will you really need me?' She had promised to spend the weekend at Angela's and she shuddered at the thought of Angela's annoyance if she turned up late.

His glance probed her face. 'Why?'

'If you could get along without me I'd be grateful.'

'What are you doing this weekend that's so important?'

She looked down. 'I'm going away, that's all.'

Suddenly she heard him breathing. It surprised her. The room was not that quiet. She looked up and saw his nostrils flaring white with the effort not to lose his temper. Natalie's eyes widened in shock and they stared at each other in silence.

'With Leyton?' he asked at last, and although his voice was even it was rough with control.

'No,' she whispered, and her own voice was shaking, because the look in his face had startled her. She looked down and spoke quickly, stammering. 'My sister is going away with her husband for a weekend, and I've promised to babysit for them. If I don't turn up, they won't be able to go.' She swallowed and tried a little humour. 'And then Angela will scalp me.'

'We can't have that,' Jake said quite calmly.

She looked up and his face was perfectly normal. The blazing, molten rage had gone from the grey eyes, and she gave a deep sigh of relief. The threat of violence which had hung over the room evaporated, leaving her weak with the memory of it. Jake was always angry when anyone tried to get out of working for whatever reason.

'So I needn't come in tomorrow?' she asked eagerly.

'I'm afraid you will,' he shrugged, and she could have killed him. Surely he could see how important it was not to ruin her sister's weekend?

'Don't be so heartless!' she burst out, and he turned a strange, sardonic look on her, his lip curling in a sneer.

'You say that to me? Don't you know what they call you here? The heartless princess.'

Tom, she thought, flushing. He had spread that nickname; it had amused him. She looked away impatiently. Angela would scream blue murder if she let her down. 'You don't know my sister,' she sighed wearily. 'I'd rather face you in your worst mood, or a shoal of angry piranha, than annoy my sister.'

He looked amused suddenly. 'She can't be that bad.'

Natalie groaned. 'She's worse. Even when we were kids she used to terrify me.'

'What does she do? Beat you up?'

She eyed him wryly. 'Angela doesn't need to use force. She can strip the skin off you at forty paces with three words.'

His eyes held enjoyment. 'Is she attractive?'

Natalie lifted her pale curved brows. 'Typical male question! Yes, she's attractive.' She gazed at him limpidly. 'Her husband thinks so, and he's six foot three in his stockinged feet and has an Oxford boxing blue.'

'Consider the question withdrawn,' Jake drawled, smiling. 'All right, when are you supposed to arrive at the gorgon's abode?'

'Tonight,' she said. 'To allow them to get away on time.'

'How old are the children?'

'Tony is four and Colin is two,' Natalie informed him.

Jake settled on the edge of her desk, surveying her. 'Well trained?'

Her eyes held derision. 'Angela's children? To a hair!'

He grinned again. 'Bring them with you to-morrow, then.'

Her mouth opened in surprise. 'You're joking!'

'Certainly not. I need you, but if you're running the risk of being scalped if you let your sister down, I'll put up with her offspring for a morning. We can always tie them to a chair.'

'You may have to. Colin is a lamb, but Tony takes after his mother.'

He laughed. 'Where does this formidable lady live?'

Natalie told him and he nodded. 'I'll drive you there after work and sum up the problem. If it's out of the question to have them around while we work I'll think of something else.' His index finger lightly flicked her cheek. 'Don't worry, it'll get sorted out.'

When he had gone she sat there in surprise staring at her desk. After being violently angry he had become quite human, indeed more human than she could remember him being since she came to work for him.

Tom dropped in later that evening and she gave him a harassed look. 'I can't talk. I'm in the middle of the timing for the last programme we edited and I keep getting it wrong.' She had dropped her stopwatch during that session and had to borrow Jake's. He had lashed her with a furious look as he handed it to her. Accidents were always happening to the stopwatches. They cost a fortune to repair and Jake was fed up with people mishandling them. Somehow the little incident seemed to have thrown all her timings into chaos and she was going mad trying to make sense of her notes.

'I just wanted to ask you to dinner on Saturday,' he said, his eyes hopeful.

'I'm sorry,' Natalie excused, 'I'm going away for the weekend tonight.'

Tom grimaced. 'Oh, well.' He strolled to the door. 'See you next week some time, then?'

'Ring me,' she said. 'At home,' adding that hurriedly because Jake got nasty when Tom rang her at work.

She had just managed to make the timings fit when Jake arrived in a very elegant formal suit and tie, an unusual get-up for him, since he usually wore jeans.

'Ready?' he asked, and she hurriedly cleared her desk before going into the cloakroom to brush her hair and do her make-up.

When she returned Jake looked her up and down with a faintly amused expression. 'I gather your sister is nothing like you?'

'Nothing,' she agreed, bringing out the little weekend case she had brought to the office.

He took it and put a hand under her arm, steering her out of the office. 'Do your parents live near your sister?'

She told him about their little house at Weymouth. 'Mother wouldn't live near Angela for a million pounds.'

He laughed. 'Poor Angela! You do give her a bad press.'

'I love her,' Natalie said. 'So does Mother. But both of us are scared stiff of offending her and when you live near one of your family and feel like that, it can be very wearing.'

'Is your mother like you?'

Natalie looked up in a surprised motion, her lashes sweeping back to leave the enormous deep blue eyes as clear as a child's. 'Why, yes. How did you guess that?'

They had arrived at the car-park in the basement and Jake guided her into his sleek white sports car. 'I guessed,' he said, winding back the hood.

They purred out of the exit into the brilliant sunshine of the summer afternoon. Natalie's hair blew wildly around her face and Jake put a hand to her cheek to brush it back. His eyes held hers. 'I like you dishevelled,' he said oddly, turning away again.

Angela stared at Jake as she shook hands with him. 'So you're the ogre,' she enunciated clearly.

Jake's brows shot up and he glanced quizzically at Natalie, who blushed. 'I was about to say the same to you,' he returned smoothly.

Angela was very quick. She looked at Natalie, too. 'I see,' she said almost menacingly.

'Is your husband really a boxer?' Jake enquired.

That surprised Angela. 'Yes,' she agreed somewhat bewilderedly.

'And six foot three?'

'And a half,' Angela nodded.

'Pity,' Jake drawled, his grey eyes moving from the sleek dark cap of her short black hair to her trim figure and long legs.

Angela laughed. She gave Natalie a sparkling look which indicated that she found Jake good company. 'Stay to dinner,' she invited him. 'There's plenty of salad if you don't mind cold meat to go with it.'

'Perfect for this weather,' he said at once.

In the spare bedroom Natalie unpacked her things while her sister sat on the bed and said to her thoughtfully, 'Attractive, you said. You didn't say irresistible. I wonder why not?'

With her back to her, Natalie slid her lingerie into a drawer very carefully before answering. 'Perhaps because I find him entirely resistable.'

'Really?' Angela sounded sarcastic, amused.

'Really,' said Natalie, turning with a defiant face.

'You say that too loudly, sister dear,' Angela drawled.

'Anyway, he wouldn't have me as a gift,' Natalie

ended, fishing out the fur mules from her case and sliding them under the bed.

'What makes you so sure?'

'He said so,' Natalie told her flatly.

Angela's eyes narrowed. 'Did he, indeed? Just in passing, I suppose?'

Natalie gave her a furious look. 'Does it matter when?'

Angela strolled to the door. 'Keep your hair on, darling. I've no intention of betraying your secret.'

'What secret?' Natalie asked hotly.

Angela smiled in her sweet, condescending fashion. 'That you fancy him like mad.'

Anger exploded in Natalie's head. As the door shut behind Angela she swore aloud, hands clenched. 'I do not fancy him,' she said to herself. 'I detest him! One of these days I shall tell Angela what I think of her. . . .' And knew she never would because, bossy and infuriating though her sister could be, she loved her and respected her, but all the same at this moment she could have got her hands round Angela's throat and squeezed her to death.

Angela and Adrian were leaving at nine and dinner had to be a hurried meal, which was why it was cold. They seemed to be getting on very well, Natalie thought, listening silently as Adrian and Jake talked about the state of the world, the tax system and how long it took to get to Heathrow airport in the rush hour. The french windows stood open at the end of the dining-room and the liquid notes of a blackbird drifted in through them.

Angela glanced at the watch on her wrist. 'We really must go,' she told Adrian, who uncoiled easily and gave her his warm smile.

'Ready when you are, angel.'

'Well, bring the cases down,' she told him, and he moved off at his loping pace to get them from upstairs. Angela glanced over the table at Natalie, who sat with her head propped in her hands, the black hair flowing over her shoulders.

'Stop dreaming and clear the table, Natalie.'

'Yes, Angela,' said Natalie, rising at once.

'I'll hurry Adrian,' her sister said, departing.

Jake grinned as Natalie began to collect the dishes. 'I see what you meant about her. Monarch of all she surveys, isn't she?'

'In the nicest possible way,' Natalie agreed. He began to help her and she gave him a polite little smile. It had just occurred to her that when Adrian and Angela had gone, they would be alone, and she wondered how to get rid of him as soon as possible.

They had just carried everything into the kitchen and stacked it in the dishwasher when the sound of Angela's scolding voice drew them to the front door. She kissed Natalie, gave her a handwritten list of reminders and smiled approvingly at Jake. The car drew away and Natalie waved until it turned the corner, then she glanced at him nervously.

'Well, thanks for the lift. I'll see you tomorrow, then.'

Angela had efficiently dealt with the problem of the boys by ringing her next-door neighbour who agreed to look after them for the morning. Jake's offer to have them at the studios had been brushed aside as absurd.

Jake strolled unhurriedly back into the house, and Natalie almost ran after him, babbling nervously. 'Thank you for the lift. I'm sure you want to get off now. It's getting late.'

'I'll help you clear up before I go,' he said as she caught up with him.

'That isn't necessary,' she said anxiously.

He turned on her, an odd hoarseness in his voice. 'What would you know about necessity?'

She backed, alarm in the oval pallor of her face, and he caught her long hair in a cruel grip, dragging her towards him. The strong, dark planes of his face had a remorseless determination. 'I swore to myself I'd never lay a hand on you again as long as I lived,' he muttered, staring at her mouth, and she couldn't move an inch as his face swooped down at her.

He hurt her and she knew it was deliberate. One hand held her throat, forcing her to stand still, and the hot, violent kiss crushed her lips until they felt numb. When at last he released her mouth she whispered angrily, 'You hurt me!'

'I want to hurt you,' he ground out through his teeth. 'I get quite a kick out of it. Cruelty to you could become an addiction to me.'

'What a horrible thing to say,' she stammered, staring at him.

'We're a long way past conventional courtesies,' Jake muttered. 'We got way past them that first night. In a few short hours I got through more emotions than I've felt throughout my life.'

His anger made her shiver, but she defended herself somehow, her voice trembling. 'I didn't mean to hurt you, Jake.'

His face went taut, a dark red colour filling the hard angles of his cheeks. 'Hurt me?' He bared his teeth furiously. 'You didn't hurt me, sweetheart, you made me bloody mad. I told you, no man with any guts could take being used the way you tried to use me. If I'd really fallen hard for you it would have emasculated me to find out why you fell into my arms the way you did.'

The tension in him was so strong that she was shaking at the impact of it, eyes scared as she looked up at him, and he saw the fear in her eyes and smiled with barbed amusement.

'Frightened, are you? So you ought to be. We're alone, and I'm seriously considering staying with you tonight.'

She tried to jerk away, quivering from head to foot, and he forcibly pulled her closer, his hands violent. 'Oh, no,' he muttered. 'Stay where I want you. And if I decide to stay my name is Jake. If I hear another name on your lips I'll murder you!'

'I couldn't help it,' she cried miserably. 'I was confused, unhappy. I'm sorry but, as you say, it was only your ego that was hurt.'

'A man's ego is the most sensitive part of him,' he said drily, sounding more controlled. 'You hit me below the belt, darling.'

She was relieved at the reappearance of his sardonic smile. The terrifying rage appeared to have gone, thank God. She gave him a quick, appealing look.

'I'm sure I didn't do any lasting damage,' she said lightly, her smile tentative, because she never really knew how Jake would react. He was incomprehensible to her. She knew so little about men, despite her marriage to Angus, and Jake was harder to read than most men, anyway. 'There are plenty of others only too eager to soothe your ego. Anthea Redmond would be delighted.'

His eyes narrowed and he watched her closely. 'You think so?' The clever face was impossible to decipher.

'She makes no secret of it.' That fact did not please Natalie, but at that moment she would have done anything to placate him, to ensure that there was no further flare-up of that icy rage which sometimes made him so violent.

His hand moved slowly up her arm, the cool contact strangely electrifying. 'All the same, I hope you know who I am now. You may hate my guts, Natalie, but you're never going to confuse me with anyone else again.'

His fingers had trailed over her shoulder to wind into her long hair, and now they suddenly tugged at it, tilting her head so that she stared dumbly into his watchful face, her blue eyes enormous, slightly alarmed. She knew he was going to kiss her, but she could not move, hypnotised by the intent stare of his eyes. He bent his head and forced her lips apart, probing them with a sensual warmth which started a languorous inertia deep inside her. Her arms slowly slid around his neck. She kissed him back yieldingly and his hands ran down her body. She felt them wandering from her taut midriff to the curve of her breast and suddenly she was groaning.

Her own hand moved against the back of his head, feeling the tension of the muscles in his nape. The thick black hair curled over her fingers as though it clung to her, and suddenly she knew she would never again mistake the back of Jake's head for that of any other man.

He buried his face in the side of her neck, his mouth burning on her skin, then he sank slowly backward on to the couch taking her unresistingly with him, and his arms pulled her closer as he found her mouth again.

The strong fingers moulded her body lovingly, their exploring path tracked by fire. She felt his touch on her with a helpless consent her mind could not deny, not even protesting when he began to slide the white dress down over her shoulders, his lips brushing lightly along her collarbone.

She was lying among the cushions with closed eyes, aware of a fierce pleasure rushing up her body, hearing the rapid beating of his heart above her as his mouth touched the exposed white breast he had been stroking. 'Who am I?' he asked unsteadily, his lips teasing her skin.

'Jake,' she moaned through lips swollen with his kisses. He took her hand and laid it against his shirt so that the heavy thud of his heart struck into her palm.

'Touch me,' he whispered, the heartbeat quickening.

She tremblingly opened his shirt and traced the powerful lines of his chest, aware of that fast deep heartbeat, hearing it accelerate as her fingers stroked the short black hair curling from his brown skin. Leaning her cheek against him, she let her lips drift down his body, the taste of his warm moist skin on her tongue and in her parted mouth.

Jake pushed her back among the cushions, gasping, his arms closing round the weak, yielding curve of her body; his black head thrust down to kiss her naked breast, the caress of his tongue on her nipples sending such wild tremors down to her nerve ends that she groaned his name, her body quivering under the weight of his.

She became aware of his thigh moving restlessly

against her, and the heat in their bodies had become explosive, a hair-trigger sensitivity to each other which might detonate at any second.

She struggled to break free of the burning passivity which held her in his arms, but he had aroused her too deeply, his stroking hands and mouth were driving her crazy, forcing hoarse little moans of pleasure out of her.

'Want me to stay?' he asked suddenly, his voice muffled as his lips probed her warm, white breast, and Natalie felt herself shuddering as she faced that question.

'Do you?' he muttered again, the exploring fingers against her thigh, and at last she groaned, 'Yes, Jake. Yes!'

For a moment he lay still on her, breathing in rough gasps, his body seeming to shiver, then suddenly he sat up and she opened her eyes in bewilderment to find him watching her with a smile so cruel that her heart missed a beat. He slowly ran insolent eyes down her half naked body and her face flamed and then went cold.

'On second thoughts, I don't think I'll bother,' he drawled, and she was stricken, wincing, filled with humiliation at the dismissal in his face as he rejected her. He watched her, triumph in his eyes, as she fumbled to dress herself again under the shaming mockery of his stare.

'That's done my ego a lot of good,' he said in that soft, mocking voice.

'Why, Jake?' she asked quietly, and the question meant: why have you done this to me? She knew she had hurt him that first night, but she had not done it deliberately, and Jake had. Just now he had acted in cold calculation, that was obvious.

'Last time it was me who got worked up to a point of insanity and then had the ground knocked from under me,' he said, and as he spoke the soft mockery went from his voice and a bitter, searing anger came into it. For the first time she saw exactly how angry he really was with her. His eyes burnt with it. 'Now you know how it felt that night I walked out of your apartment with a knife wound in my guts,' he said.

Natalie stared, neither moving nor speaking, the delicate lines of her face quite immobile. Jake stared into the dark blue eyes, probing them for a reaction.

She was fighting desperately to keep the pain out of her face. She made her eyes stay steady, breathing carefully, struggling with the feelings he had deliberately inflicted, and he watched her with a raw eagerness he made no effort to hide.

'Beg me to stay, Natalie,' he murmured. 'I might if you made it tempting enough. Of course, that's not what I came for, but I could be persuaded.' The grey eyes flicked over her insultingly. 'Oh, yes, I could be persuaded.'

Nothing would have persuaded her to let him now. Nobody in her whole life had ever deliberately set out to hurt and humiliate her before. It would kill her to have him touch her again.

Because he loathed her. Hated her. It was in the grey eyes, in the hard cold lines of his mouth. A moment ago that mouth had driven her crazy as it moved against her body, and now she looked at it and felt sick.

The worst part of the pain was buried in the back of her mind and she refused to let it surface, but it stayed there all the time, on the periphery of her vision, tormenting her.

'Say something, damn you,' he muttered suddenly, his voice raged with anger ... and she silently shook her head.

She had nothing to say to him, now or ever. She held her sleek dark head high, the oval medallion of her face pale between the flowing strands, and moved towards the door. She opened it and stood back, holding the handle, making it clear that he should go.

For a full moment Jake stood there, his face tormented, eyes glaring at her.

Then he smiled coldly. 'Maybe you're right. I've got what I came for. In any case, I've got a date with Anthea, and although she's a very passionate lady she has a temper to go with it.'

He walked past her. She heard him going down the hall, heard the front door open and close quietly. Then there was the sound of his car door being closed, still in that controlled fashion. A few seconds later the engine leapt into life.

He drove away and as he went Natalie felt the blood draining slowly from her limbs and she began to shake so badly that she thought she might fall down. Shock, she thought vaguely. She was icy cold with it.

Was this how it had felt to him that night? She had heard that when a limb was amputated one could feel a shadow pain for weeks afterwards although the limb had gone. That was how it would feel to her for a long, long time.

Stiffly she walked to the whisky decanter and poured herself a stiff drink. She had never drunk the stuff before with any pleasure. Now she swallowed the glassful and felt the heat run round her

Could <u>you</u> dare love a man like this?

Leon Petrou was wealthy, handsome and strong-willed, and used women merely to satisfy his own desires. Yet Helen was strongly...almost hypnotically drawn to him.

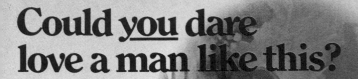

Could <u>you</u> dare love a man like this?

YES, eavesdrop on Leon and Helen in the searing pages of "Gates of Steel" by the celebrated best-selling romance author, Anne Hampson. She has crafted a story of passion and daring that will hold you in its spell until the final word is read.

You'll meet Leon, Helen and others, because they all live in the exciting world of *Harlequin Presents*, and all four books shown here are your FREE GIFTS to introduce you to the monthly home subscription plan of *Harlequin Presents*.

A Home Subscription

It's the easiest and most convenient way to get every one of the exciting *Harlequin Presents* novels! And now, with a home subscription plan you won't miss *any* of these true-to-life stories, and you don't even have to go out looking for them. You pay nothing extra for this convenience, there are no additional charges …you don't even pay for postage! Fill out and send us the handy coupon now, and we'll send you 4 exciting *Harlequin Presents* novels absolutely FREE!

Harlequin Presents…

ANNE HAMPSON
gates of steel

JANET DAILEY
no quarter asked

ANNE MATHER
sweet revenge

VIOLET WINSPEAR
devil in a silver room

Mail this coupon today!

body with relief. A silent scream was echoing in her head.

Jake had deliberately, coldly humiliated her to get revenge for her own quite innocent humiliation of him.

And at this moment she couldn't even hate him, only feel pain widening in her body in ever-increasing circles until she was nothing but agony from head to toe.

The anger came later when the pain had lessened a little. Oh, God, she thought wildly, I'd like to kill him. She planned various deaths for him in mental slow motion, but none of them was satisfying enough. The rotten swine, she thought, grinding her teeth. Then it hit her. She would have to go in tomorrow and face him with that between them. Her hands covered her face. She couldn't. She couldn't do it.

He would smile and there would be nothing, absolutely nothing she could do about it. Every flick of his grey eyes would be flaying the skin from her.

She thought feverishly for a way out. Tom, she thought. His name was like a saving hand held out as she went down for the final time. She rang him, hand shaking. He sounded surprised but delighted to hear her voice.

'Tom, do you like children?' she asked, and he gagged before he answered.

'Are you proposing to me?' His voice had laughter in it.

'Only a visit to the zoo tomorrow,' she said lightly, delighted with her own ability to sound so calm.

'Come again?'

'I'm babysitting for my sister this weekend. I told you I was going away, didn't I? Well, her two little boys want to go to the zoo. I just thought. . . .'

'Zoos are my favourite places,' he said. 'Where shall I pick you up?'

'I've got to work tomorrow morning,' she said easily. 'Could you call in at the audio room on floor one? Say, twelve-thirty?'

'Darling, I'll be there on the dot,' he said.

When she hung up she looked at herself in the mirror. Her blue eyes had a glazed wildness which shook her. Whatever it cost, though, Jake Lang wouldn't see her flinch tomorrow. She was going in with flags flying and with a bit of luck she could act well enough to make him think the deliberate wound he had inflicted on her was merely a pin-prick.

He was in the audio room when she walked in there next day. She had chosen a very feminine powder blue silk dress, the lines of it soft and gentle, seductively clinging, giving her slender figure a curved outline. The sound mixer looked round and whistled appreciatively and she smiled at him, a brilliant warm smile which brought quick response from him.

Somehow she retained the smile as she glanced briefly at Jake Lang. He had his head lifted, a pile of tape in his hand, and she caught a fleeting glimpse of the surprise in his eyes. What had he expected? That she would crawl in here, a whipped and defeated creature? He could think again!

She picked up her stopwatch and clipboard and sat down beside the sound mixer, crossing her legs, knowing that both men were watching the smooth movement.

'Where's my script?' Jake barked.

Natalie gave the sound mixer a confidential little

smile. 'In your case, I imagine, Mr Lang.'

'Get it,' Jake snapped.

She put down her stopwatch and clipboard slowly and carefully, stood up and walked across to the large leather case. Jake watched her every inch of the way. She found the script, turned and walked back to him, her face bland. She handed it to him with another of those sweet little smiles.

'Headache, Mr Lang?' she asked sympathetically. 'Shall I get you some coffee and aspirin?'

'Sit down,' he ground through his teeth.

It was the same throughout the morning. The mixer grinned at her from time to time, winking. 'Bad case of the morning after the night before,' he whispered.

'Yes,' Natalie agreed, smiling.

At twelve-thirty on the dot Tom sauntered in and Jake turned and looked at him with murder in his eyes. Then he looked at Natalie.

'Hi, Jake,' Tom said cheerfully, apparently unaware of the ice in the other man's face. He slid an arm round Natalie and smiled down at her. 'Ready, darling? I can't wait. As I said last night, I thought you'd never ask.'

''Bye!' they called brightly as they left, but the only answer was a faintly disconsolate one from the sound mixer. Jake didn't say a word.

The day at the zoo was fun. Natalie laughed a good deal and let Tom walk them round every square inch of the place. They bought souvenirs and orange squash and stood in awed horror in front of the glass cage of alligators in the aquarium. Tony said thoughtfully, 'If I had all those teeth I could eat six dinners.'

'Eight, I'd say,' Tom argued.

'Or ten,' Tony said triumphantly.

'Or a dozen,' said Tom, not to be outdone.

'Don't be silly,' Tony jeered, glaring at him. 'And anyway, Mummy wouldn't let me.'

'That's true,' Natalie nodded. Angela certainly wouldn't.

'I could eat two dinners, though,' said Tony, eyeing Tom. 'I bet I could.'

He did. Tom watched with awe as he finished Colin's egg and chips. 'Where does he put it?'

'In my stomach, silly,' Tony said derisively. 'I've got a picture of a stomach.'

'Ugh!' Tom groaned in disgust.

Eyeing him with calculation, Tony added, 'With food in it.'

Tom pushed away his plate. 'Shall we go?' he asked plaintively.

'Chips and beans and sausages,' said Tony, enjoying himself. 'You've gone all green.'

'You horrible little monster,' Tom muttered. 'I'd like to put you in the alligator case.'

By the time Tom drove them back to Angela's house, Natalie felt as though every bone in her head was aching with fatigue and pain. But she had to keep up a pretence of gaiety. She cooked Tom a dinner and sat with him listening to a lively Billy Daniels tape from Angela's collection of music. Tom slid an arm around her waist and kissed her. She felt faintly sick but she did not protest. She would never again feel a man kiss her without this wrenching sensation of pain, she thought.

When Tom went at last she was exhausted. The effort of appearing bright and happy had used up all her energy and she fell into bed like someone who hasn't slept for weeks. In the dark room she turned her face into her pillow and would not cry. Some pain was too deep for tears. When they told her Angus was dead she had not shed a single tear. She had merely shrivelled inside as if her body had been plunged into searing flame. Lately she had begun to feel she was coming back to life. She had woken without that old, dragging heaviness. She had smiled and talked to people. She had been on her way back to life and Jake had savaged her so badly that the shadows had closed round her again, and this time she did not think she would ever want to climb out of them again.

CHAPTER SIX

NATALIE went in to work on the Monday not certain what to expect, but armoured for anything, and now the bitter enmity was out in the open. Jake looked at her with hatred which knifed her every time their eyes met, and his temper was brittle, easily aroused.

The others commented freely on it to her, their faces rueful. 'Talking to Jake these days is like walking through a minefield,' one of them said. 'Just now I asked him where you were, and he bit my head off.'

Natalie retained her cool smile. 'Why did you want me?'

'The slavery file,' the researcher groaned. 'I've lost it again. Have you seen it?'

She found it and he left, smiling, a smile which died as Jake met him in the door and gave him the sort of look that goes right through your breastbone and out the other side. The man visibly flinched and vanished like a rabbit into a burrow when it sees the fox.

Jake slammed the door on him and turned to look at her. 'Would it be too much to ask you to do some work now and then, or do you think I pay you to sit in here flirting?'

There was no answer to that, so she bent her head over her work without a word. Jake walked round to his own desk and sat down, glaring at her. 'Book me a channel for seven tonight,' he snapped.

'Yes, sir,' she said expressionlessly, wishing he would go out again because having him sitting there was driving her mad, infuriating her; she couldn't bear to have him facing her, the hard lean body in her angle of vision, his slight movements attracting her eyes all the time even though she fought the temptation to look at him.

It drained her, this constant fight. It took every scrap of her energy, all her willpower.

She talked to the rather impatient woman in Bookings and had a long wait while the schedules were checked and re-checked on the other end of the phone before a triumphant voice announced, 'No, we can't fit him in at seven.'

There was always a log jam of people wanting studio space, rehearsal space, tape channels. Natalie was accustomed to argument, the need to coax and persuade, even to beg. She launched into one of those long campaigns, but got nowhere. Jake suddenly got up, came round and took the phone from her. 'Now listen,' he barked into it. 'I want a channel. Understood that?' A confused mumble. 'I don't give a damn. I must have it!'

He got it. He slammed the phone down and his grey eyes held a brilliant anger as he looked at Natalie. She looked away, returning to her work. Jake worked in silence opposite her, but that terrible tension quivered between them all the time, an electricity which others could feel when they ventured into the room from time to time.

Natalie had arranged to meet Carol for lunch. She was relieved to get away from the atmosphere in the office and lingered over the meal, reluctant to leave. Carol gasped, looking at her watch, 'I'm late, I must run. Come on!'

'Go on without me,' Natalie said on impulse. 'I've got some shopping to do.'

Carol glanced at her curiously but said nothing. Everyone knew how Jake Lang reacted to unpunctuality, but Natalie's pale face had a set determination which precluded argument. Carol shrugged and went, leaving Natalie to follow in her own time.

She took her time, wandering around the shops and staring at clothes, perfume, jewellery, without seeing much of any of them. When she finally arrived back at the office she was an hour late and people were waiting in the office for her, members of the research team with teasing eyes who, after asking where she had been, said, 'J.L.'s in a tearing rage.' She coolly dealt with their problems without commenting on that. They left and she began work, concentrating hard.

She knew he was back before he entered the room. Her spine tingled. The door was flung open. He stood there for a few seconds, then it crashed shut.

'Where the hell have you been?' he asked grimly.

'Looking for another job,' she returned, lying, and yet knew that that had been in her mind all the time as she walked around the shops.

Jake stood at her shoulder without speaking for a moment. 'I might have known that would be your answer,' he said levelly. 'Running; like the little coward you are.'

'What did you expect? I'm not working with you any longer than I can help.' Natalie had lost her own temper now. She was wound up, her tongue free, and she turned to face him with flashing eyes.

'Have you any idea what a swine you are?' She caught the sardonic movement of his mouth and her temper burnt higher. 'No, I'm not just talking about your attempt to humiliate me sexually the other night. I'm talking about your nasty temper in the office, your sarcasm, your savage tongue. The way you stride around cracking a whip, not just over me but over everyone unfortunate enough to work for you. Do you think it makes you popular? You expect us to work longer hours than anyone else, yet you're rarely civil to any of us. You snarl and snap even when things go well, and when they get difficult you're impossible. The others say you're just going through a bad patch, that although you've always been tough to work for you aren't always a complete swine. They're ambitious, they stay because they want to do the job badly enough to put up with you and your foul moods. But I'm not putting up with it—I'd rather work in the salt mines. I hate your guts!' She said the last words on a fevered note, her hands clenched. 'I can't stand the sight of you and I'm getting out of here as soon as I can.'

Jake stared. When she had stopped shouting he just stood there and stared at her, and the cold grey eyes moved slowly from her overheated skin to her brilliant eyes and then down to her angry mouth. Her colour deepened even further under that look.

'Well, well,' he drawled on a strange note, his brows rising steeply. 'So you've suddenly found a tongue. I must have put quite a sharp thorn in that cold little heart to get a reaction like that.'

'You couldn't touch my heart in a thousand years!' she flung back furiously, her hands curling into talons as though she would run at him and rake her nails down his smiling face.

'Don't dare me, Natalie,' he said, leaning towards her. 'I'd have thought by now you'd know I always pick up a gauntlet.'

'I know you're contemptible,' she retorted, suffocatingly angry now, aware that she could scarcely breathe with all that emotion clogging her throat.

He studied her through half-closed eyes. 'Calm down,' he murmured. 'It's fascinating, though.'

'What is?' she asked coldly, trying to force back the hot rage which still flooded up inside her at the sight of him.

'To see you like this,' he said, his mouth sardonic. 'There's something about that cool little face of yours that makes me want to rip the mask away from you, but I never suspected it might hide a temper as explosive as this.'

Natalie gave a rough sigh. 'I've never lost my temper like that in my life before.' The dark blue eyes glared furiously at him. 'It took you to drive me mad.'

Jake gave a strange sharp sound, a rapid intake of breath, and moved away to stare out of the window. She watched his lean back and wondered if, somehow, she had got home a dart. She hoped she had. She hoped she had penetrated his thick skin.

He turned and looked across the room at her. 'You're the best secretary I've ever had. In a few weeks you've become the pin that holds the team together. Do you think I haven't noticed the way they all come in here to chat and ask advice? Every time I walk in the door there's someone in here bringing you their problems. The girls come and weep on your shoulder, the men come in to get your sympathy. For a quiet little mouse of a girl you have an incredible amount of magnetism. I suspect it's your very quietness that brings them. You say so little and you listen so well. They always know they can get your ear.'

He was astonishing her. She couldn't believe her ears. It was true that the others often came to talk, but she had not realised Jake had noticed that.

He stayed where he was on the other side of the room, watching her unguarded face. 'We make a good team,' he murmured.

Her eyes opened wide and his lips twisted at her open surprise.

'Hadn't that occurred to you? You say I crack a whip and I don't dispute it, but I'm in a hurry and I have to drive them all. When it gets too much for them they scuttle in here to sob out their troubles to you. They come out cheerful and get back to work. You're their safety valve.' He paused, his eyes on her. 'You're my safety valve.'

Natalie looked back at him incredulously.

'However tough I get I know I can trust you to soothe them back to normal,' he explained coolly.

'You mean you use me to ...?' She could have hit him. 'How dare you? That's the most....'

'Unscrupulous?' He suggested as she paused to seek the right word to convey her detestation. 'Despicable?'

'Oh, you're very good with words,' she bit out. 'You're so clever, Jake. You can run rings round me with that tongue, but I won't let you use me in a cat-and-mouse game with the others!'

'Hell, it's not a cat-and-mouse game,' he said impatiently. 'What do you think would happen if I let up and left them to work as they chose? Oh, some of them would work hard, but most would settle into a life of sloth. They don't like work, they want to enjoy themselves. They need someone behind them with a whip. Sure, they hate me at times. My hide is tough, I can take that. And when I've blown them up they can come to you to be calmed down. It works. Surely you realise that since you came we've got on twice as fast?'

She had not known. It had never occurred to her.

'I won't let you resign,' he said flatly. 'I need you.'

'I don't give a damn what you need,' she retorted, but her voice lacked conviction because he had undermined her. He had altered her picture of things. She suspected it had been deliberate. Jake was so clever with words, he could twist them, manipulate them, slide them into one's mind in some sort of sleight of hand one never noticed. He had made her feel ridiculously flattered by what he had said. True or not, it had made her feel wanted, needed, appreciated. She looked at him ruefully.

'Of course you care,' he said, and now he came closer, his deep cool voice filled with amusement. She did not want to look up into the grey eyes, but she found herself doing so, struggling to retain the memory of pain, trying to hate him. He was smiling, his mouth crooked, and her heart turned over at the charm in his face.

'We all like to be needed,' he said. 'I've no doubt it would give you a great kick to walk out on me at the moment, knowing I depend on you, but you can't do that to the others, can you Natalie? You're far too kind. You have a strong sense of responsibility. You care about people. You told me what a bossy little madam your sister is, but what you didn't tell me was how much she needed you.'

Her eyes rounded. 'Angela?'

'Angela,' he mocked, smiling. 'I saw how she leans on both you and that quiet husband of hers. Oh, yes, she bullies you both, pushes you both around. But I saw her face light up when you arrived. I saw her smiling at her husband. We're all interdependent, Natalie. The team have grown to need you and you couldn't bring yourself to walk out on them, could you?' His grey eyes were wicked. 'Not leaving them to face me without your sweet, silent protection?'

She looked down, confused by his expression, unwilling to let her disturbed senses sway her brain. The cruelty of his behaviour the other night was fading like a bruise on healing skin. 'You're a swine,' she said faintly.

'Hate me, then,' he said close beside her. 'But don't go.'

She still hesitated and he put a hand under her chin, lifting it, tipping her face towards him. The blue eyes were very dark and puzzled, uncertain.

'Are you going to demand an apology, is that it?' He grimaced. 'I behaved like a swine—I'm sorry. You'd have to be a man to understand the scar you left on me the night we met. It put me in a blazing temper and with you working next to me all these weeks I haven't been able to forget it. I was aching for some sort of revenge. Being cruel to you was like cauterising a wound with a hot iron. It took away the pain.'

He had eased his own pain by hurting her, she thought wryly, understanding only too well. He felt she had humiliated him, so he had humiliated her, forcing her to want him and then walking out on her.

'Can we wipe the slate clean and start again?' he asked quietly, staring into her eyes, trying to read the thoughts behind the dark blue gaze. 'We work well together. I find you invaluable here; I don't want to lose you. We can never be anything but colleagues, I realise, but at least we could work together in some sort of harmony if we just forget everything that's happened between us.'

Forget? she thought. Did he imagine she could do that so easily? No man had ever treated her the way he had. She couldn't forget that.

'Don't go dumb on me again,' he said impatiently. 'What do you say? Will you try again?'

'As colleagues,' she said slowly.

'Just that,' he nodded curtly, face hard. His mouth took on that sardonic, crooked mockery. 'Neither of us wants anything but a calm working relationship. I can forget the rest, if you can.'

Could she? Natalie wasn't sure. But she enjoyed this job. She liked working here. Jake had given her a sense of involvement by what he had said and although she guessed he had been carefully deliberate in flattering her like that, it had been balm to her wounded pride, a salve which was already removing the sting he had inflicted.

'Very well,' she said, 'I'll try.'

He straightened, moving away. 'Fine. Now get me the timings on the second programme. I want to check them through with you.'

The rapidity with which he moved from the personal to the businesslike amused her. She found the folder and they sat down to go over the timings together. Within ten minutes Natalie had forgotten everything else, involved in the work.

Her explosion that day altered their relationship.

Jake's temper was calmer, less brittle. Although he still roared and snapped from time to time he was often reasonable. He still expected the utmost effort from them all, kept them working long after they might have gone, chivvied and bullied anyone who did not seem to be working well, but the vicious sting rarely came into his voice. The whole team noted it and relaxed.

He had done most of the filming over in Africa, but there were necessary parts left to be filmed in Europe, welding clips which he had left to the last so that he should be certain exactly where they were needed. 'We'll do those when the rest is in shape,' he told her. 'It will involve trips to Belgium and France, certainly, possibly Holland.'

Natalie found herself far less tired after work these days. She was seeing a good deal of Tom in the evening and at weekends. He was a lively, relaxing companion and she liked him a good deal, but she knew he never probed beneath her surface, tried to discover what made her tick, as Jake had. He was satisfied with her as she was on the outside. It delighted him to see men turn and glance as she walked past with him. He talked and Natalie listened and if that was unsatisfying to her, Tom never seemed aware of any lack between them.

All the same he was kind, an even-tempered young man. What woman could be fool enough to prefer a man who wrung from one the extremes of emotion, hurting and exhausting, a man who could offer hell as much as heaven, and with whom one would probably never know a quiet moment?

Not me, Natalie thought. That sort of love could leave scars. She already had one or two and that was enough.

Anthea Redmond did not seem scarred, however. She seemed to take Jake Lang in her stride, her superb self-confidence undented by any of his tempers, if she ever saw them. With her, he seemed warmly at ease. He was always with her. Natalie caught glimpses of them in the canteen, saw them leaving together after work, heard that they were seen together all the time. 'They're laying bets on it,' one of the team confided to her.

'On what?' she asked, although she immediately did not want to know.

'How long it lasts and whether it ends in a wedding,' she was told. 'Anthea seems sure it will, but Jake Lang's a very cagey bird. He's steered clear of marriage until now and it's my guess he'll go on doing so.'

Natalie shrugged, her oval features bland, and the other looked at her with a grin. 'I know, he leaves you cold. He doesn't have that effect on others. Anthea's the most envied girl in the place.'

'She doesn't have to work for him,' Natalie said grimly.

'God, that's true. Although he's not so bad since you came. You seem to soothe the savage breast.'

When the man had gone she stared at her typewriter. Soothe the savage breast, did she? A lot he knew!

Summer swung into a lazy, somnolent peak and the whole of London went mad, spending long hours lying in the green parks, the policemen on traffic duty in their shirt sleeves, the girls in sleeveless cotton dresses and the men with open shirts. Life down in the bowels at Metropolis was murder. The heat seemed oppressive in the studios and recording rooms. Nobody had much energy or enthusiasm for work when the temperature climbed to the eighties in the shade and the pavements sent up waves of heat as one walked on them.

One Saturday morning Natalie and Jake spent two hours desperately trying to cut pieces of film which all seemed essential yet some of which had to go. Jake's black hair stood on end at the back where he had wildly run his fingers through it and his voice was hoarse from irritation as he sank back in his chair at last. 'It will have to do,' he said grimly.

They went up in the lift and emerged on the ground floor. The enormous plate-glass windows of the foyer glittered like fine crystal in the sunlight and Jake shielded his eyes with a groan. 'My God, it's hot! What I'd give for a few hours at the sea.'

Natalie closed her eyes, sighing. 'I know what you mean.' Images of blue water sighing up on sandy beaches filled her mind, then she laughed. 'The coast is probably hectic today. The beach will be packed like a sardine can.'

'Horrible realist,' he muttered. 'Like a lift?'

It never occurred to her to refuse. 'Thank you,' she said, and followed him down to the car-park.

As the car moved slowly through the mass of Saturday traffic in the city he drummed his fingers on the wheel impatiently. 'Seeing Tom today?'

'He's over in Brussels,' she reminded him. 'Doing a piece on the Common Market.'

Tom came and went like a homing pigeon, his job sending him around the world, and it was half his attraction for her since he was as often away as he was here, yet everyone had them paired now and it left her free from other advances.

Jake shot her a quick look. 'I know a quiet swimming pool,' he said softly.

She smiled briefly. 'On a day like this it won't be quiet. Nowhere cool will be.'

'This will,' he said. 'My mother has one in her garden.'

It surprised her. 'Your mother?'

His eyes held mockery. 'Did you think I wouldn't have a mother? Imagined I'd been made out of bits of barbed wire and concrete, I suppose?'

Her mouth curved in amusement. 'The thought did occur.'

'No,' he said. 'Unlikely as it seems, I have a mother. A father, too. He was a lawyer, but now he grows roses. Millions of them. And my mother has a swimming pool.'

She gave him a suspicious look. 'Are they likely to be at home today?'

His grin was derisive. 'Yes, my wary little bird, they're at home, both of them, and they expect me to lunch. Join us.'

'I couldn't do that! You can't just spring an uninvited guest on your mother, especially on a day like this.'

'Why not?' he asked coolly. 'We're having salad and there'll be plenty to spare. She wants to meet you, anyway. I've mentioned you to her and she's curious to see the human lynch-pin in person.'

She blushed, half smiling. 'You're absurd!'

'We'll stop off at your flat to get your swimsuit and then we can spend the afternoon in nice cool water.'

Natalie sighed, irresistibly drawn to the idea. If she stayed at home there was just the weekend housework to be done, the tidying and writing of letters, the solitary meals and silence.

'Be tempted,' he murmured softly, watching her out of the corner of his eye. 'I've an idea you'll like my mother, and my father will certainly like you. He has an eye for beauty, especially still, silent beauty. That's why he adores roses. The house and garden are full of them. He'll insist on showing you the ribbons and cups he's won with the damned flowers, but I'll drag you away before he bores you rigid and you can spend a few lazy hours in the pool.'

'Why does your mother have a swimming pool?' she asked. 'Does she use it much?'

'Daily,' he said, nodding soberly. 'She had polio twenty years ago. We thought she would die, but she pulled through, largely due to my father, I think. He just wouldn't let her go. Afterwards she was paralysed, though. A therapist advised swimming to strengthen her muscles. It took three years, but now she walks as well as ever she did, although with a slight limp. And she swims every day.'

'How could she swim if she was paralysed?' asked Natalie, deeply interested and moved by his story.

'My father lowered her into the water and held her. She just floated for a long time, but gradually she found herself moving. As I said, it took years, but my God, it was worth it.'

'Your parents sound marvellous,' she said, looking at him with a lift of her fine brows.

He grinned with wicked amusement. 'Well, say it.'

'Say what?'

'That you can't imagine how they got a swine like me for a son.'

Natalie found herself smiling involuntarily. 'Well, I can't.'

'No, tough luck on them,' he agreed. They pulled up outside her flat and he said quietly, 'Run and get your swimsuit, Natalie.'

She fought a brief battle with her common sense. They had formed a strong working relationship, but it was dangerous to allow any personal one to start up again between them. He read her expression and waited in a curiously deliberate way, watching her.

She looked up at the deep, burning blue sky and thought of the cool water lapping around her overheated body. It was tempting. . . .

'Stop fighting me,' he ordered. 'You'll enjoy meeting my parents and you've been working damned hard for weeks. Relax, girl.'

She gave him a half smile, half sigh. 'Very well.'

An hour later he turned into a pair of apple-green gates and purred up a short drive between rhododendron bushes in full, gorgeous flower, their blue and pink and purple tropically vivid and improbable.

The house was square and built of creamy stone, the line of the roof crazily rising and falling, with gables making it comically individual. As Jake parked near the front, a door within the gabled porch was opened and three dogs raced out, barking. He climbed out and grinned as they surrounded him, leaping up to lick his hands, wagging their tails and visibly adoring him.

'Stop it, you fatheads,' he told them mock sternly. Natalie stood quietly watching him and he looked up to grin at her, the black hair windblown around his powerful features.

'You're late, as usual,' said a soft warm voice, and Natalie turned to see a very thin, small woman in the porchway.

Jake kissed her lightly, then indicated Natalie. 'Guess what I've brought you, Mother.'

A pair of gentle blue eyes met Natalie's and the fine-featured face softened into a smile of welcome. 'So you're Natalie,' the woman said, and in surprise Natalie glanced at Jake. How on earth had she known? Or had he mentioned that he might bring her? Had it not been an impulse after all? Had he planned it?

'I'm Elizabeth Lang, Jake's mother,' the soft voice went on. 'As my graceless son sees no reason to introduce us. You must call me Elizabeth, not Mrs Lang, though. I feel I know you too well for formality.'

Natalie could not repress the start of surprise and Elizabeth laughed quietly. 'Oh, Jake talks to me. I know sons aren't supposed to confide in their mothers these days, but when I was so ill I think we fell into the habit, don't you, Jake? It was so dull in my quiet little room. Jake came clattering home from school and it was fascinating to hear all about his day. He and his father saved my life by bringing the world to me when I couldn't go out to see it.'

'He didn't tell me that,' said Natalie. 'He told me his father had made you live.'

'They both fought like tigers,' Elizabeth said lightly. She was a slightly built woman, tiny beside her tall son, her bones delicate, her hair totally white but long and fine, tidied away into a loose bun behind her small head.

She glanced at her son now. 'Your father is a little out of temper because you're late. The lunch has been waiting for half an hour. I told him the traffic would hold you up, but you know how impatient he gets.'

Natalie's eyes smiled as she listened and Elizabeth caught that look and laughed. 'Oh, yes, that's where Jake gets it from. I often feel sorry for myself, caught between the two of them.'

'I hope it isn't too inconvenient to have an uninvited guest for lunch,' said Natalie as they walked round the house towards the garden stretching at the back.

'Not at all,' Elizabeth assured her. She walked lightly yet with a distinct limp in one leg, Natalie noticed. 'There's plenty of salad, boiled eggs and cold meat. I only wish I'd known Jake might bring you—I would have got a more elaborate meal.'

'In this weather, nothing could be more delicious than salad,' said Natalie gently.

Then she halted, gasping, inhaling the unbelievably heavenly fragrance of the garden. 'Good heavens! How lovely.' Her eyes swung across rows and rows of rose trees, their blooms softly glowing among the leaves, their perfume quivering on the heated summer air. 'Jake said you had lots of roses, but I hadn't imagined this in my wildest dreams.'

'My husband is an extremist,' Elizabeth said drily. 'He likes roses, so he grows roses. In their thousands. I doubt if even he knows how many he's got. Yet if I ask permission to cut a bloom or two for the house he flies into a positive rage. The men of this family are fiercely possessive, I'm afraid.'

'Roses belong in a garden, not a vase,' said a deep voice, and they all turned towards the new arrival.

Natalie regarded him with amazed curiosity. She would have known on sight that he was Jake's father, she thought. He was an older version of his son, his body very wiry and lean, like whipcord, his skin deeply bronzed by hours in the open air, his hair as white as his wife's yet with Jake's thick profusion and making her suspect that once it had the same shining darkness.

He came towards them, moving casually, wearing old tan cords and a tan shirt open at the neck, and smiled at Natalie with the same lack of surprise his wife had shown. His eyes were the same grey, a little lighter, perhaps, but penetrating, sharp, taking in everything about her.

'Dad, this is Natalie,' said Jake, and he put a hand on her arm as he spoke, a curious little gesture which sent a quick pang through her.

She shook hands with Mr Lang and congratulated him on his garden. 'Your roses are superb. The scent is heavenly.'

'Yes,' he said without mock modesty. 'You like roses?'

'Very much,' she said. 'My father grows them too, but his garden is very small. He would be delighted with yours.'

'I hope he'll see it some day,' he said, smiling. He glanced at Jake. 'You're late. Where the devil have you been?' He had the same brusque way of speaking, she thought. It was incredible how alike they were.

'I'm sorry,' said Jake. 'The traffic was heavy and I had to take Natalie to her apartment to get her swimsuit.' He gave his mother a grin. 'I lured her here with a promise of a swim after lunch.'

'Not immediately after lunch,' Elizabeth said. 'But when she's relaxed for a while of course she must try the pool.'

The lunch was leisurely and delicious. They ate

on a terrace at the top of the garden, their heads
in the shadow of a fringed umbrella which fluttered
faintly above the table. The deep sweet scent of
the roses, the sound of the birds, made it a mem-
orable meal. Elizabeth and George Lang talked
to Jake and Natalie sat listening without saying
much, her oval face dreamy between her soft black
hair. She was utterly content. The heat had receded
a little while they sat beneath the shade of the umbrella. The day seemed to her perfect here, an in-
credibly lovely afternoon in high summer. Occasionally one of the others looked at her and she
smiled, her curved pink mouth gentle in repose, her
blue eyes unconsciously sweet.

Jake talked about his work, glancing at her from
time to time, mentioning her name in passing.
George Lang told his son about the latest rose show
at which he had taken prizes. Elizabeth talked about
a book she was reading, a petit-point foot-stool she
was embroidering. There was a coal-tit swinging on
a string bag of peanuts among the close-set leaves
of a lilac tree near the terrace and Natalie watched
it sleepily.

Afterwards she offered to help clear and wash up,
and Elizabeth smiled her thanks. They worked
while the men sat talking. It impressed Natalie to
realise the depth of the bond between parents and
son. Here Jake was utterly different from the slave-
driver of the office. His voice held that deep, calm
certainty. His face was strongly at ease.

This was his home, she thought. He had an apartment
in London, she knew that, at which no doubt he
spent most of his time. But this was home to him,
wherever he might live. She felt it as she saw the grey
eyes roam contentedly over the massing rose trees

and heard him talking in that lazy voice to his father.

'Tell me about yourself,' Elizabeth invited as they worked in the immaculate kitchen. It was a modern yet traditional room, the units a pretty green with chrome handles and fittings, the fringed blinds a delicate yellow which gave the room a sunny, spacious warmth. It must be fun to work in such nice surroundings, Natalie thought.

Aloud she said, 'That's a difficult question, Elizabeth. Where does one start?'

'Your marriage,' said Elizabeth, and the question made Natalie gasp in surprise and shock.

It had brought sharply into focus something of which she had been aware but which she had not thought too much about. In the last few weeks she had been cut free, not from Angus, but from the pain of losing him. The dead haze in which she had lived after his death had lifted. She thought of him now with a gentle, loving regret, but the agony had gone. Angus would aways be a part of her, but now she had a life in which he had no part at all.

She turned almost bewildered blue eyes upon Elizabeth. 'Did Jake tell you?'

Elizabeth dried her hands, watching her. 'Do you mind if he has?'

That depended, Natalie thought, on just how much he had told. But surely he wouldn't tell his mother everything? Her face glowed with colour as she said, 'I'm not sure.'

'Does it still hurt?' Elizabeth asked, gently, without probing too deeply.

Natalie's eyes flickered nervously. 'Not as much. I think I'm getting used to the idea of being without him. Eighteen months is a long time. We only knew each other for two years—almost as long as the time since he died.'

'What was he like?' Elizabeth asked.

Natalie sighed. 'Rather like Jake—to look at and in character. Strong, determined, clever. I never knew what he saw in me.'

'You were happy together?'

'Very,' Natalie said.

Elizabeth's eyes went past her suddenly, a frown coming into her face. Natalie turned just as the kitchen door swung shut. She looked at Elizabeth. 'Was that Jake?' She was not sure why she felt it had been, but for some reason it disturbed her to think he might have been there, listening to her talk of Angus.

Elizabeth looked at her carefully. 'Yes,' she said. 'How do you get on with Jake in the office? I imagine he's not easy to work for.'

Natalie smiled drily. 'Not the easiest boss, no.'

'He's very like his father,' Elizabeth told her. 'They're both extremists, possessive to the point of being bloody-minded and wildly romantic.'

Natalie's eyes opened wide. 'Romantic? Jake?'

Elizabeth watched her. 'He hides it better than his father does, but yes, he's a romantic, a dreamer under that hard-headed exterior, with a strong leaning towards the very fanaticism he claims to despise.' She laughed. 'He makes fun of his father's love for roses, but he has the same tendency to go mad over things.'

Natalie remembered that as George Lang showed her round the garden. 'You must take some roses back with you,' he said, watching her appreciative face with pleasure. 'Which would you like?'

'Oh, the dark red velvety ones,' she said at once, smiling.

He glanced at her with a masculine glint remarkably like Jake's smile. 'You ought to like the white ones. They remind me of your beautiful skin, my dear.' And laughed when she blushed.

When they rejoined the others Jake gave his father a wry smile. 'You've monopolised her long enough!' George Lang eyed him teasingly.

She was surprised to see a flush come into Jake's face, then he stood up and asked: 'Are we swimming, or not?'

They walked down to the swimming pool together, leaving his parents on the terrace. The water had a glittering blue invitation which was irresistible on a day like this, the sun dancing over the surface in dazzling points of light. There was a tiny changing room in which she changed first while Jake sat outside. He stared openly as she emerged and she felt herself flushing. The white one-piece swimsuit was pretty and demure, yet she felt uneasy under his slow inspection.

'Very modest,' he mocked as he went to change. Natalie lowered herself into the water, sighing with pleasure at the cool stroke of the water on her heated body.

Jake suddenly dived in from the side, cutting the air in a perfect arc, and she felt a peculiar dryness in the throat as she watched his body enter the water. He surfaced close beside her and without a word swam strongly away. Natalie floated on the water, eyes closed, enjoying the lazy sensations of feeling the sun on her wet body while she gently drifted along.

Jake startled her by appearing just below her,

tugging at her feet, so that she sank beneath the water, struggling.

'You scared the life out of me!' she spluttered as she surfaced again, pushing damp strands of hair out of her eyes.

'It's good for you to be shaken up,' he said, quite unrepentant. 'You have a tendency to drift into daydreams which annoys me.'

'Nobody who works with you needs shaking up,' she retorted. 'You're like dynamite—you explode at the least touch.'

He grinned, the grey eyes amused. 'I'm glad you've noticed.'

They trod water together, her eyes wandering over the brown, muscled power of his shoulders and chest before they came up to meet his watching gaze with a sense of nervous shyness. The sun was already drying the moisture on his shoulders and they gleamed with a golden smoothness which made her long to touch them. His eyes narrowed as though he could read her thoughts and she turned in something of a panic, swimming away.

He came after her and caught at her trailing wet hair with a grasp which wrung a cry of pain from her. 'You're hurting!'

'I told you,' he said roughly, 'I enjoy hurting you.'

Natalie was shaken at his tone. For weeks now they had seemed to reach a balanced calm between them, a long truce which she would hate to see wrecked, and his words came as a shock, revealing that under his friendly exterior the enmity still smouldered.

He still held her hair and suddenly he wrenched at it, forcing her head back until it floated on the water, face upward, then he bent his head and kissed her with a cruelty which made her gasp. The pitiless mouth ground her lips back upon her teeth until she tasted the salt of her own blood on her tongue. She pushed at his bare, wet shoulders, her hands sliding on his moist skin, and he slid his arms right round her body, his thighs entangling hers, his kiss softening and deepening. Natalie melted helplessly into a sensuous response, kissing him hotly with closed eyes, the naked brush of their bodies closer and closer, the cool water sliding round them as they shuddered convulsively.

Suddenly like a knife through the heart came the knowledge that her love for Angus had never sent this hunger burning through her veins. She was pulsating with it, her arms now round his neck, her hands caressing his wet head, stroking his hair. She had not believed it possible that any man could do this to her. She had not been aware that she was capable of a desire so fierce, so consuming.

The realisation woke her from the heady excitement Jake had bred in her. She broke away, breathing hard. 'No,' she groaned, and swam to the side of the pool.

He did not follow. She clambered out and ran to the changing room, bolting the door with trembling fingers.

A feeling of betrayal filled her. She had wanted Jake just now with a need which shamed her. No thought of Angus had even reached her. Jake had dominated her thoughts, her feelings, her body.

Shaking, she sat down on the slatted seat and stared at the wet pool her feet had left on the floor.

My God, she thought, I'm in love with him.

CHAPTER SEVEN

How had it happened? When had it happened? Natalie sat there, shivering slightly, searching her memory and trying to pinpoint the moment when this emotion had taken possession of her.

Not that first night, she thought. That night Angus had been the only thing in her mind. Jake had been a shadow which resembled the man she needed, wanted.

At some time after that she had begun to feel attracted to him in his own right. The night he made love to her at Angela's house she had responded to him, to Jake, without a thought of Angus, but by then she was certain she was still not in love. It had been a purely instinctive physical response she offered him, a reluctant feeling which had died at his cruel humiliating rejection.

No, her emotional involvement had *begun* that night. Jake had stabbed her and for some reason it had brought her fiercely awake. The cold dream in which Angus's death had left her had gone in those moments. Gradually over the past weeks she had been falling in love with Jake. The seed must have been present in her the first time they met, but she had never known it for what it was, and Jake's treatment had given it a beanstalk growth. The hatred she had convinced herself she felt had been the dark side of an emotion which was slowly filling every part of her.

She covered her face with her wet, trembling hands. She had to be insane. In love with Jake Lang? Only a fool would be.

Pulling herself together, she dried herself and dressed, fingers fumbling with zip and belt, her teeth chattering as though she were frozen, but it was shock which had chilled her body, not the temperature.

Stepping out into the brilliant sunshine left her blinking, dazzled. Jake climbed out of the pool and padded towards her, his wet feet leaving an impression on the concrete. Natalie avoided his eyes, pushing her damp hair away from her face.

'I'll go ahead,' she said coolly.

He caught her arm, his fingers light. 'Natalie, I'm sorry.'

She glanced at him then, the dark blue eyes wary.

'I promised to keep my hands off you, I know.' His face had a hard wryness which hurt. 'The trouble is you're very beautiful and I'm not good at self-control. Lovely women are a temptation I find it hard to resist.'

'Well, try,' she said curtly, pulling her arm away and walking away. Charming! she thought furiously. He might think it flattering to call her beautiful, but it was certainly no compliment to be told he treated all attractive women the same. Not that she needed to be told—he had a reputation for it. Gossip had preceded his arrival. He was the sort of eligible bachelor who evades pursuit while enjoying himself to the full. Anthea Redmond might have a chance with him; she had a hide like an elephant herself. Jake was going to find it hard to shake her off. That thought pleased Natalie. Then she bit her lip. Why lie? It didn't please her, it made her sick. She could not stand the thought of him touching another woman.

His mother tried to persuade her to stay to dinner, but she pleaded a necessity to go home and when Jake joined them, his black hair drying already in the heat, Natalie told him she had to go.

His face was expressionless as he nodded. 'I'll drive you back.'

'There's no need,' she said quickly. 'I can take a taxi. It will spoil your weekend to have that drive twice.'

'I brought you,' he said brusquely. 'I'll take you home.'

'Come again soon,' said Elizabeth, watching them with a shrewd and thoughtful expression.

George Lang had cut her an enormous bunch of red roses, their smooth petals deeply perfumed. He handed it to her and then gave her one white rose, a perfectly formed blossom which made her eyes shine. 'You're very kind,' she said, holding it to her nostrils. 'What delicious scent!'

Jake placed the red rose carefully in the back of his car. Natalie held the white rose in her hand as he started the engine and waved her free hand to his parents.

Jake did not say a word as they drove. She sat there, her hair blown round her face, feeling the coolness on her hot face, glancing down at the long-stemmed white rose now and then with a sensation of pleasure.

When Jake pulled up outside her apartment he half turned and glanced at her, his arm lying along the steering wheel. 'Thank you for coming. I'm sorry

I spoilt the day. I'd hoped you would stay for dinner.'

She looked down, fiddling with her rose. 'I have a lot to do. Thank you, though. I enjoyed meeting your parents.'

'They enjoyed meeting you,' he said, and leant over to pick up the rose, lifting it to his face. She watched his mouth hover over the waxen white petals, watching him breathe in the perfume. He lifted his eyes and looked at her, then trailed the flower deliberately across her warm cheek until it touched her mouth. Her heart began to beat wildly. She could not hold the grey eyes. She looked down, blushing.

'Don't let my stupidity spoil your relationship with my mother,' he said quietly. 'She doesn't often take to people the way she took to you. I was sure you would like each other. Will you go and see her now and then?'

'I'd like to,' she said huskily.

'That gentle sweetness of yours is just what she needs,' he said. 'They lead a very quiet life and you fit it perfectly.'

She could not stand it. She pushed at the door and Jake got out and came round to help her out. He put the roses into her arms and she muttered a farewell before diving away.

She stood in her apartment later and looked round at the roses. They filled three vases, their perfume giving the stuffy little room a heady sweetness. Jake's gentleness was harder to accept than his savagery. He did not want her for herself; he wanted her as a friend for his mother. Her mouth writhed. No, she thought, he wanted her; she had known that when he had her in his arms in the pool. Even if he had not made it plain from the start. But it was a physical hunger which she had no intention of satisfying, even though it might feed her own needs to do so.

She thought she would find it hard to face him in the office on the following Monday, but in fact she was knee deep in work when he arrived and barely noticed him, and after that everything was normal. They lapsed back into the working relationship which she found easier to bear and Jake never gave a sign of anything else.

Tom came back from Brussels with a pretty Belgian doll for her, the white-capped head demure above a full, embroidered dress. She had it on her desk when Jake walked into the office. He glanced at it, picked it up. 'Tom?' he asked evenly, and she nodded. 'I heard he was back,' said Jake, putting it down. It fell off the desk and she heard the china face crack as it hit her metal wastepaper basket.

'Oh!' she exclaimed, running round to pick it up.

'Have I broken it? I am sorry,' Jake said with all the marks of genuine contrition. 'I'll get you another.'

'It doesn't matter,' she said, inwardly mourning the pretty little thing.

'You can't have a doll with a broken head,' Jake pointed out, and dropped it into the wastepaper basket. 'I'll get one exactly the same. Tom will never know.'

Natalie stared at him, incredulous. He walked out of the office and she heard him shouting at one of the researchers. Bending, she picked the unfortunate doll out of the pile of wastepaper and flicked ash from people's cigarettes. The team tended to use her basket as an ashtray, and there was ash all over the doll's clothes and face. It had been perfect, delicate, enchanting. Now it had a smear of blue carbon on its nose and a grubby look from the ash.

He did it deliberately, she thought. There had been a savage satisfaction in the way he dropped the doll into the wastepaper. Why? Her skin heated. Jealousy? He had never shown signs of it before. Surely not.

Unless Jake resented the fact that although she had denied him she had gone out with Tom a good deal. Maybe he thought she was sleeping with Tom. That might account for it.

Her poor doll! Tom would be so hurt if he saw it. She hid it in her bag and Jake came back and glanced into the wastepaper basket and then at her, his eyes sharp.

He said nothing and neither did she. They went on working and the phone rang, the team came in and out, and at the end of the day Natalie went off with Tom to the cinema, but did not confess to him what fate had befallen his present.

A few days later Anthea Redmond came into the office when Natalie was alone and gave her a cold smile. 'Jake about?'

'I'm sorry,' said Natalie. 'He's having lunch with someone and won't be back until three-thirty.'

Anthea shrugged. 'I'll see him later.' She showed no sign of going, however, lighting a cigarette and lingering, watching as Natalie went on with her work. 'Still dating Tom Leyton?'

'Yes,' Natalie said briefly.

'So long as you leave Jake alone,' Anthea said sweetly.

'I'd leave him alone on a desert island,' Natalie said with a vicious snap which surprised herself.

Anthea looked delighted. 'You funny girl,' she

drawled, purring, and wandered off.

Natalie worked late and Jake came in at around seven with a frown so black that it made her heart sink. He had not looked so angry for a long time, but now he asked her icily why she was still there, adding, 'Go home. I'm sure Tom's waiting for you.'

She shrugged and stood up. 'Actually he flew off to Stockholm at two o'clock and won't be back for a week.'

'Too bad,' Jake bit out.

Natalie should have gone, but she hesitated. 'Is something wrong?'

'What should be wrong?' he asked nastily. 'Everything's perfect.'

She saw there was no point in trying to propitiate him, so she walked to the door. Jake stood with his back to her as she went out and did not say goodnight.

Swine, she thought, then miserably, what was the matter with him? He swung like a weathercock. She never knew how she would find him. Lately they had been almost at peace in their relationship, then suddenly this outburst.

It was when she was in her bath that she suddenly heard the telephone ringing. She would have ignored it, but it went on and on, so she climbed out and wrapped a towel around her. Dripping, she answered it and Jake practically yelled, 'Have you got the time sheets with you?'

Natalie jumped, mind blank. 'What?'

'For God's sake, you stupid little bitch, have you taken the time sheets home?' he roared.

'Don't talk to me like that!' she yelled back, and heard him gasp.

'Who the hell do you think you are, bellowing at

me?' he asked with a snarling rage which came down the phone at her as though he wanted to hit her.

'I think I'm a human being who's just been called foul names, and I won't stand for it,' she retorted as angrily.

There was a silence. 'Natalie, have you got the time sheets?' he asked after a moment.

'I don't think so, but I'll check my bag,' she said.

They were not in her bag. They were in her pile of magazines. She remembered now gathering the magazines up before she left the office so hurriedly. The time sheets must have been underneath them and she had brought them away with her.

Grimacing, she picked up the phone as gingerly as though it might bite her. 'I'm sorry. Yes, I must have picked them up by accident. I'll bring them back faithfully tomorrow,' she said.

'I need them now,' he said angrily.

Natalie looked down at her dripping self. 'I've just got out of the bath to answer your call,' she protested. 'I can't come back to the office now.'

'Then I'll come and get them,' snapped Jake, slamming the phone down.

She looked at her own phone with a wrathful expression. He really was the limit! One day I'll hit him, she thought. Then she dried herself and dressed hurriedly in a sleeveless linen dress of a slightly darker shade than her eyes. She had just blow-dried her hair when he leant on the bell and went on leaning on it until she yanked open the door.

He eyed her glitteringly, his face grim. 'Where are they, then? I haven't got all night. I'm working.'

'Maybe that's what's wrong with you,' she

snapped. 'You ought to knock off now and then. It's almost ten o'clock and you were at work when I arrived. You must have been at work for nearly twelve hours.'

'I can count,' he said unpleasantly. 'Where are those damned time sheets?'

She turned and walked across the room to get them and he closed the door, leaning against it, his arms folded.

She came back with the time sheets in her hand. 'Have you eaten?' she asked. 'Maybe your blood sugar is low. You ought to break for a meal before you start work again.'

'The canteen will be closed until midnight, remember,' he said coldly.

'You could surely get a snack somewhere,' she protested.

'Are you offering me one?'

She had not been, but she shrugged. 'I suppose I could find you something simple.'

His mouth was tight. 'This is as close to a desert island as we're likely to find, remember.'

She stared. 'What?'

'Forgotten you said it?' The grey eyes were savage.

And then she remembered and flushed, eyes falling away from him. Anthea had repeated her remark, no doubt with suitable embellishment. Was that what had put him in this vile mood?

She nervously gave him a quick look. 'I'm sorry, Jake. She made me angry and I just snapped back.'

'Why did she make you angry?' His eyes had narrowed and she felt herself flushing more deeply.

Why not tell the truth? she thought. Blow Anthea. 'She warned me to leave you alone,' she said limpidly, watching him through her lashes.

He came closer, staring. 'And that made you angry?'

'I don't like being warned off as if I were a trespasser on a private estate,' she said. 'Are you going to marry her?'

Jake pushed his hands into his pockets. 'Marriage is in my mind,' he said softly.

That sent a shaft of such pain through her that she had difficulty suppressing a groan. She bit her lower lip, then hurriedly turned away. 'What would you like to eat? I could get you some salad or an omelette.'

'Omelette sounds fine,' he said, following her into the tiny kitchen. 'I am starving, now you mention it.' He watched her get down eggs and crack them into a bowl before beating them lightly. As she sliced butter into the pan and poured them in he said: 'Next time Anthea provokes you don't say things she can repeat to me.'

'I'm sorry,' she said, sliding a palette knife under the golden circle and flipping it deftly. 'You should have asked me instead of turning into Attila the Hun.'

His hand touched her back, slid slowly down the curve of her body. 'Are you planning to marry Tom?'

'He hasn't asked me.'

'Don't quibble. You know he'd ask you if you wanted him to.'

Natalie laughed, turning the omelette out on to a plate. 'Is it that easy? Can you see me ordering him to propose?'

'You wouldn't need to,' he said, sitting down at the tiny table. She put the plate in front of him and swung away to make some coffee. He ate slowly and with obvious enjoyment. 'You,' he said softly, 'are a fantastic cook. Among other things.'

'I like cooking.' She laid out cups and he finished his meal and sat back to watch her.

'Did you cook for him?'

She was puzzled. 'Who?'

Jake stared, eyes narrowed. 'Your husband.'

She felt herself flush. 'Oh. Yes, of course.'

Jake looked down at his empty plate. 'You're getting over it, aren't you?'

Natalie was silent, watching the bubbling of the percolator. He leaned back over the chair, making it creak in protest, his arms behind his dark head in a lazy stretch.

'Aren't you?' he insisted.

She nodded, turning off the coffee. 'Black or white?' she asked him.

'Black,' he said. 'I've got work to do.'

'You ought to leave it. Does it matter whether you do it tonight or tomorrow? Why are you working so hard?'

'I always do,' he shrugged. 'It's the way I'm made. No half measures.'

You can say that again, she thought, pouring his coffee and then her own, adding cream to her cup before sitting down at the table. He inhaled the scent of the coffee with eyes closed and then said, still with eyes hidden, 'You look half alive to me, whether you're getting over it or not. What you need is a love affair, and I don't mean the milk and water thing you have going with Tom Leyton. He hasn't done a thing to you.'

There were pulses beating at her throat and wrist, but her voice was steady, to her relief, as she answered. 'What makes you so sure?'

Jake lifted his lids lightly and she saw the gleam of the grey eyes through his lashes. He looked amused. 'I've got eyes.' Then he smiled and her stomach turned over. 'I could make you forget him if you let me.'

'Drink your coffee before it gets cold,' she said huskily.

'You know I could,' he murmured. 'We've proved that. Do I still remind you of him?'

'No,' she whispered.

'Even in the dark with my back to you?' His face had a wry self-mockery as he spoke.

Natalie shook her head. In the dark with his back to her if he was a mile away she would know it was Jake. She could scarcely believe she had ever mistaken him for anyone but himself.

'You're emotionally anaemic,' he said coolly, watching her. 'You need an injection of good red blood.'

She was conscious of very dry lips and a closed throat. Getting up awkwardly, she knocked over her chair. She bent to pick it up and as she straightened found him standing beside her. 'Don't touch me,' she said in a shaking voice.

He ignored her, his hands closing round her face, his thumbs pushing into her hair, the grey eyes watchful as he looked at her. 'You're very beautiful,' he said quietly. 'But you could be even more beautiful if you came to life. You're like an android, Natalie, lifeless, perfect but not quite human.'

Stung, she snapped angrily, 'I'm human!'

He shook his head. 'No, you need a love affair to bring those blue eyes to life. I almost feel blasphemous when I touch you, as though no living man had a right to put a hand on you, and that's no way for a woman to be: I'd like to see your face after I've made love to you for an hour or two. I can't believe you'd look as sweetly untouchable as you do now.'

'If I'm ever in need of a man I'll find my own,' she said coolly. 'I know the popular theory about widows. Do you think you're the first man to imply that I'm desperate for love? I'm not, I assure you. I'm perfectly happy as I am. I'm not in the market for a lover.'

His face tautened and the grey eyes held a chilling anger. 'Cold as charity, aren't you? I'd like to knock that restrained little smile off your face.'

'You did that a long time ago!'

His mouth curled contemptuously. 'Oh, I made a slight dent in your icy surface, but not enough for me. I want to see the ice crack right across.' The powerful hands tightened and he bent his head to find her mouth before she could move away. She fought, shivering under the ferocity of the kiss, aware of rage under his controlled manner.

'You just can't get over the fact that it was Angus, not you, I wanted that night,' she said, pulling free.

His eyes darkened with temper. 'Last time it was me,' he said thickly.

'Last time you walked out on me,' she flung back.

'I must have been crazy,' he said, his lips drawn over his teeth in a tight snarl. 'I had a mad idea of getting my own back, and in a way it did wipe out the sting of knowing you only wanted me that first time because I looked like him, but it didn't stop me wanting you, and I cursed myself for letting you go when I could have had you. I find frustration very hard to take.'

'How sad,' she said mockingly.

'Don't provoke me,' Jake whispered, watching

her. 'I can become violent.'

'Don't I know? Working with you is like living on the slopes of Mount Etna!'

'Be careful you don't get burned, then,' he muttered. 'One day there'll be a really volcanic eruption between us, Natalie. Twice before I've been on the point of getting you into bed, only to be frustrated. Remember the old tag—third time lucky.'

'Not if I see you first,' she bit out angrily, her face very flushed. The memory of the last time was only too vivid in her mind. How dared he talk about her as though he only had to stretch out a lazy hand and he would find her falling into his possession like a ripe fruit?

He grinned, suddenly restored to good humour. 'I'll have to make sure you don't see me coming, then.' There was mocking humour in his eyes. 'Because I am going to have you, Natalie. Make no mistake about that.'

Yes, she thought, so that you can wipe out for ever the memory of my first night with you, erase that humiliation which your ego finds so unendurable. Even having humiliated me in turn hasn't quite wiped it out. You need a total victory to do that.

She gave him a cool little smile which masked her secret thoughts. 'Thanks for the warning.'

'It won't do you any good,' he returned lazily.

'No?' She looked at him expressionlessly. 'We'll see.'

'Yes,' he said thickly, 'we'll see. And when I've shattered the ice behind which you're hiding, Natalie, I'll sate myself with you.' The words were spoken hoarsely and made her shudder, her eyes widening at the tone, the phrasing. He didn't move to touch her, but his eyes were deadly. Their touch on her body was like fire. She winced as though that look burnt her. 'I've waited too long to be satisfied with anything less,' he added after a moment.

He turned and walked out, and she stood in the empty flat looking round it with eyes that saw nothing.

He still hated her, she realised. It was a strange devouring hatred, but it was hatred, all the same. Love did not cloak itself in words like that. Oh, God, she thought, closing her eyes. It would be like going over a precipice to let him touch me again. I would fall and fall and be smashed to pieces. Even if he loved her, she was not the sort of girl who went in for love affairs, and knowing he hated her made it a hundred times worse. He would not just harm her; he would scar her, maim her, leave her with the taste of ashes in her mouth. Men could enter into an affair lightly and forget it. Women's emotions always became involved. When the affair was over they were the ones left feeling sick and miserable. They could not escape it. They could not separate heart and body.

When a woman gave herself she gave everything, cursed with a need for permanence, needing to love as she needed food and drink. Natalie had learnt about love and loss the hard way, but at least when she grieved for Angus she had known that with them it had been a mutual warmth, a caring emotion which only death had ended. Even knowing how deeply Jake could already affect her she knew she could never accept less from him. If she let him have his own way he would destroy her. Indeed, she sensed that nothing short of her destruction could satisfy him. It had lain in his eyes as he looked at her, a murderous desire to consume everything that was alive in her. Jake's ego had been lashed badly and it had bred in him a need to reduce her to a cipher, to drain her life away in order to feed his own.

CHAPTER EIGHT

NATALIE had learnt long ago to disguise her basic shyness behind a quietly pleasant mask, and she was to be grateful for that over the next few weeks. She needed all her self-possession under the mocking observation of those grey eyes. Jake missed no chance to make the matter plain, not only to her, but to everyone around them. He did not touch her, but he looked at her, and the way he looked at her made her shiver and made the rest of the team look embarrassed. If he had made love to her publicly he could not have been more obvious.

Natalie had two choices. She could either speak sharply to him, react in anger, or she could give him no opportunity to make capital out of the situation and remain apparently blind.

She chose the latter, sensing that Jake would get less mileage out of that. He was, of course, expecting her to lose her temper, say something, do something. Then he would have moved a step further; she was sure of that. So she said nothing, did nothing. She merely looked at him emptily, her face polite, and she went to lengths to make sure they were never alone.

It was easier because they were so busy. There were members of the team coming in and out all day and nothing Jake could do about that. So he lounged at his desk and stared. While she talked to people she felt the grey eyes moving over her as if they ate her. People looked at him and did a double take, at first. Then they carefully did not look, and that was worse.

Because, of course, they looked at her instead, and their eyes were curious, enquiring. They wanted to know what effect Jake was having and she needed all her acting ability to hide that from them.

Within twenty-four hours it was all round the building. The grapevine worked more efficiently than anything else at Metropolis. Natalie felt eyes on her back as she walked into the canteen and almost walked out again, but she had learnt her lesson now. She looked blandly at people and smiled as though she had no idea what they were talking about.

Tom's absence made it easier because none of them dared to put the question to her directly. They smiled. They hinted. But they did not quite dare to ask because Natalie had a quiet dignity which silenced their curiosity.

Carol was the first to dare and she did so obliquely, giving Natalie a careful look first. 'How's Jake?'

Natalie stiffened. 'Fine,' she said in light tones. 'Breathing blood and fire as usual.'

'But not to you?' Carol smiled coaxingly, hopeful of confidences.

Which, Natalie thought cynically, she would rush off to broadcast around the place at once. Aloud, she said, 'To everyone. He's very democratic. We all get it in the neck.'

'Of course,' Carol murmured, watching her. 'He's always fancied you, hasn't he? From that party. I guess he got mad when you preferred Tom Leyton to him. Not surprising. I mean, Tom's sweet, but he isn't Jake Lang.'

'That,' Natalie said drily, 'is his chief asset.'

Carol did not believe it. Wide-eyed, she shook her head. 'You're crazy! Jake Lang is God's gift to women.'

'Who told you that? Him?'

Carol giggled and put a hand to her mouth, taken aback, glancing over her shoulder as though caught in some blasphemous act. 'How can you talk about him like that? Everyone fancies him. Anthea Redmond is nuts about him.'

'Anthea Redmond is welcome to him.' Natalie looked carefully bored, pushing back the stray tendrils of long black hair with one lazy hand. 'I wouldn't have him as a gift if he came wrapped in tinfoil.'

'Why don't I get your chances?' Carol sighed. 'I'd grab him like a shot!'

'You'd regret it,' Natalie retorted. Carol didn't know him; she had no idea of his capacity to be cruel. She could not confide in her, though. There was no one she could trust to listen and understand.

Later, she was to regret having been as frank with Carol as she had been, anyway, because of course it all went back to Jake.

He walked into the office like a wind from the steppes, his eyes homicidal, and slammed the door shut right in the face of one of the team. Natalie looked up, startled, catching the man's surprised, curious face before the door closed on it.

Warily she glanced at Jake, but he was already beside her and his hand hurt on her throat as he gripped it. 'You talk too much,' he muttered blackly, his thumb pressing into her throat as if he wanted to squeeze her windpipe until she stopped breathing.

That was one accusation no one had ever levelled at her before, and she half smiled, which made him angrier.

'Funny, is it?' he asked. 'Then laugh this off!'

He almost suffocated her, his mouth bruising her lips, and she did not have to put up a fight against him because the brutality of the kiss hurt her too much to be enjoyable. She merely sat there, limp and cold, while he forced her mouth in a protracted rape which made her furious with him.

Jake drew back at last, breathing thickly, and glared at her. 'So you wouldn't have me as a gift?'

'No,' she muttered, giving him an icy stare. 'Not if you came covered in diamonds.'

He brushed that aside, his eyes staring into hers. 'You'll have me,' he bit out. 'Believe me, Natalie, you will. The longer you fight, the more I'll enjoy it when I get you. And you can repeat that to your town-crier friend whenever you like.'

Carol had wasted no time, she thought. Why did I ever let her lure me into discussing him? Won't I ever learn?

To Jake she said, 'I'll type it out if you like and pin it on the notice board. I'm sure the team would like to be the first to know your intentions.'

He smiled unpleasantly. 'Oh, I think they already know, don't you?'

'You've left them in little doubt,' she agreed icily.

He shrugged. 'They were not my main target.'

No, she thought, I was. 'I told you that you were a swine once before,' she said quietly. 'I understated the case.'

'You flatter me.' He even looked as though he

thought she did, too, and that annoyed her even more.

'I wouldn't have thought your ego could take such a public display,' she hit back.

He grinned lazily. 'The more public the better.'

That puzzled her and he read her surprise in her blue eyes, looking at them with mockery dancing in his face.

'When I finally get you, they'll all know,' he said very softly, and her eyes fell away, as something else occurred to her. Of course! She had publicly rejected him in the beginning and he meant her final capitulation to be just as public.

'You calculating swine!' she whispered.

'Thank you.' He laughed as though she had flattered him again. He touched her cheek with one finger. 'Don't keep me waiting for too long, Natalie. I'm not a patient man.'

'Then you'd better learn some patience,' she retorted with ice in her eyes, 'because you'll wait till Doomsday!'

His eyes ran down her body and she felt the heat rising in her veins. 'It might even be worth it, at that.'

After that little incident she backed out of every conversation which seemed likely to mention Jake, however casually. Now she knew that every word she said about him was red-hot news. It meant that her manner had to become even more withdrawn, but she was used to that.

Tom rang her the evening he got back. Warily she waited for him to mention Jake, but she soon realised he had not yet heard. They had dinner and talked cheerfully.

When Tom kissed her she was stiff, her face worried. Sooner or later he was going to hear about Jake. She was not sure how he would react, but she did not want him to think she was using him in any way. Tom was becoming too fond of her and although it had been clearly understood that theirs was a friendship without strings she felt responsible for the growing affection she saw him offer her.

'Tom, I like you very much,' she began, and he cut lightly into the sentence.

'I know how it goes on, Natalie. The ghastly word "but" always comes in somewhere. You don't need to tell me that.'

She smiled. 'We did say no strings.'

'We did—I remember it vividly.' Tom grinned at her. 'I promise you, Natalie, there are no strings.' He gestured with his hands. 'See? Not one.'

'Even if it were not for my memories of Angus I'm sure I couldn't love you in that way,' she said uncomfortably.

'Did I ask you to?' He sounded slightly angry now.

'I'm sorry,' she said quickly.

'Forget it.' He leaned over to open his car door. 'Goodnight, Natalie.'

She had been clumsy, she thought, hurting him when there was no excuse, and she wished she could recall the words. Tom was very nice. His kindness had been a great help to her, and now she had hurt him.

What would he think when he heard the gossip which was top of the charts at Metropolis?

Before she could find out, however, fate took a hand. Angela rang her early next morning as she was dawdling over a cup of coffee before leaving for work. 'Can you take over here for a few days?' she demanded in her usual brisk tones.

'Is something wrong?' The request was unusual enough to put some anxiety into Natalie's voice.

'Would I ask if there wasn't?' Angela sounded irritable, yet there was a distinctly unhappy note somewhere in her voice and Natalie's anxiety grew.

'What's wrong, Angela?' she asked gently.

A pause, then Angela said flatly, 'Adrian has to go to New York and I have to go with him.'

That did not sound so terrible, yet there was still that impression of unhappiness lingering in Angela's voice, so Natalie tried again, patiently. 'Why?'

It came out then, rapidly, impatiently. Adrian's firm were sending him to America for two years. It was promotion and he felt he could not refuse, but the American side of the firm insisted on vetting not only Adrian himself but Angela. 'They take the view that wives are an important part of the job. Who do they think they are? Running a tape-measure over me like this?' Angela's pride was hurt and that was part of what was bothering her, but there was far more to it than that. Under Natalie's loving probing it came out at last. Angela did not want to leave England. She did not want to leave her family.

'I wouldn't see you for years,' she said roughly, determined not to show any softness.

'When do you want me to come and take over?' Natalie asked.

'Right away,' said Angela. 'The firm suggested I send the boys to Mother, but you know she couldn't cope with them. Colin, perhaps, but not Tony. He'd run rings round her.'

Natalie smiled. 'Yes,' she agreed. Mother was too gentle for a tough little egotist like Tony, she thought. 'I would have to ask Jake for time off.'

'He'll give it,' Angela dismissed, casual where such things were concerned, unwilling to believe that anyone had anything more important than her problems on their mind.

Natalie made a face. She didn't know Jake. When she had rung off she looked at the telephone. Would he be at his apartment? She had his number somewhere. After a quick search through her address book she found it and dialled the number. The telephone rang for a long time before it was snatched off the hook and a thick, impatient voice asked, 'What?'

She suppressed a smile. 'Mr Lang?' she asked in her most civil tone. 'Natalie Buchan here.'

A silence succeeded that. Then he said slowly, 'Well?'

'An emergency has come up. Could I have a week off from work?'

'What sort of emergency?' he demanded.

She quickly explained and he grunted irritably. 'Why can't she get someone else to do it? You're my secretary, not her nurserymaid.'

'She's my sister!'

'What has that to do with it? I pay your salary to have you keeping my office afloat, not to go dashing off to dance attendance on your sister's kids.'

'I'm sorry if it inconveniences you,' Natalie murmured.

'You sound sorry,' he retorted. 'What if I say you can't go?'

'I hope you won't,' she replied quietly.

'Do I detect a threat, Natalie?' His voice was nearer, a note of odd intimacy in it. 'What would you do if I refused?'

'Go,' she said coolly.

'Daring me to do my worst?' he laughed softly. 'You have a gun at my head, have you?'

'I don't know what you mean.'

'You know all right.' She heard him yawn. 'Okay, get back as soon as you can.'

He didn't even say goodbye. The phone just clicked and he was gone. Natalie looked at the receiver in her hand with a wry face. Typical. He really was the most maddening, irritating man.

Later that day she kissed Angela goodbye as Adrian put their cases into his car, teasingly saying: 'I hope you're taking your chic black suit. That will knock their American eyes out!'

Angela lifted her chin in a defiant movement. 'Oh, I mean to, don't worry. I won't have them using me as an excuse to mark Adrian down.'

'You'll petrify them,' said Natalie, and was not altogether joking. Angela in all her warpaint could be a terrifying sight. Strong men had been known to blench and women definitely trembled. 'I suspect you'll get on in the States like a house on fire,' she told her sister.

'If it's what Adrian wants I'll grin and bear it,' Angela retorted. 'But I shan't like it.'

Natalie hesitated. 'You'll be charming to them, won't you, Angela? You can be when you like. If you're hostile it could lose Adrian this job, remember.'

Angela looked at her impatiently. 'I'm not a ninny!'

'No,' Natalie laughed, kissing her.

Angela's arms tightened in a brief hug. 'Wish me luck.'

.'My fingers will be crossed every minute of the time,' Natalie promised.

Angela drew back, resuming her confident, bossy mask. 'Don't let Tony eat anything he shouldn't. No snacks between meals. And no crisps or sweets, however much he begs.'

'No,' Natalie promised, smiling.

'Watch Colin when he has his bath, too, because he drinks the water.'

Natalie nodded. Angela had left her the usual long list of warnings, but there were always last-minute flurries of anxiety to cope with, so she listened soberly, not bothering to point out how experienced she was at dealing with her nephews.

When they had gone the two little boys stopped crying as if someone had turned off a tap. Cunningly they begged for milk and biscuits, a forbidden treat, and Natalie gave Tony a grin.

'I've been warned about you,' she teased.

'Just 'cos Mummy's gone away and left us,' he pleaded, eyes still wet.

She got her hankie and gently dried his face. 'What do you think Mummy would say?'

He knew only too well what Mummy would say. He gave her a coaxing smile. 'Just this once!'

'Famous last words,' she commented drily. Colin gave a little snort and she looked at him hard. He was very small, she thought, his face pink and damp with tears. 'Oh, come on,' she grinned. 'Mummy will have my ears for this!'

Whooping, they settled around the kitchen table and grazed on the biscuits she provided.

'You're my favourite auntie,' Tony confessed, snuggling up to her.

'I'm your only auntie,' she pointed out, her arm

holding him close to her shoulder.

'If I had lots you'd still be best,' he promised, and she grinned.

When both of them were tucked up in bed asleep she settled in front of the television and sewed buttons on Tony's old pyjamas which still fitted but had lost their buttons during a pillowfight with Adrian. Angela was far too careful to throw anything away if it could be used and the work basket was full of cast-offs which no longer fitted Tony but which would be useful for Colin later.

There was a peculiar warmth in sitting there doing things for the two children while they slept peacefully upstairs. After watching a popular comedy series and a documentary about Hongkong Natalie tidied away her work and went up to have a bath and wash her hair, falling into bed later without any of the obsessive images of Jake which had kept her awake night after night lately.

When she woke up she found two small, warm bodies bouncing on her and groaned. 'What time is it?'

'Three o'clock,' Colin said at once.

'Don't be silly,' contradicted Tony. 'It's breakfast time.'

'How do you know that?' Natalie asked gravely.

' 'Cos I'm hungry,' he returned.

'But you always are!'

'Breakfast sort of hungry,' he explained. 'And the milkman's been and Mr Grey's gone to work, so it must be breakfast time.'

'Well, clear off and let me dress, then I'll get your breakfast,' she promised him.

The boys ran off and she dressed. Going into their shared bedroom she found Tony dressing himself clumsily, his buttons misplaced so that his little shirt looked comical. She undid them and put them into their right holes while he chattered, then she dressed Colin, who still retained that baby fragrance of talcum powder and milk somehow, his small body soft and cuddly.

They ate their cereal in a ritual race, the first to reach the Rupert Bear at the bottom of their bowls getting a prize, they claimed. She gave them each half an apple which they ate while she cleared the kitchen. Buttoning them into their cardigans, she sent them out to ride round the garden on their tricycles while she did the housework and prepared their lunch.

'My very very favourite,' Tony smiled when he saw the fish fingers on his plate.

The day passed pleasantly. Natalie felt the memories of her own life fade as she became more and more involved in looking after the two boys. She was finding it hard already to think about the office, the complicated procedures of the job, the tension of Jake's pursuit of her.

The tranquil moments of the day came closer and closer together until she felt she had never done anything but what she was doing now. Looking out of the kitchen window at the quiet garden all the tensions of her other life fell away. This was another world. How many worlds are there? she wondered. Each human being carried his own world inside his head and it seemed so permanent, so real, until he moved out of it and into another, which was just as real, leaving one with this strange sense of impermanence and insecurity. Life was like a shifting kaleidoscope of colour and sound. Impressions whirled inside one's head and were gone.

There had been something totally concrete and permanent about her love for Angus, but he had gone, taking with him a whole universe of love and involvement for her.

She had thought she would never get over it. Day by day she had lived with grief until her nature was imbued with it, steeped in it, as though that dark stain spread through her whole being.

Then Jake had exploded into her life and the kaleidoscope had shifted again.

I love him, she thought, and no longer fought the realisation. He is real to me now, even though he was a dream shadow when we first met, and whatever happens he will always be real to me. All the worlds in which people moved were real. They were impermanent by nature. Life is finite, temporary. Only love was infinite. Her love for Angus was not over; it existed in its own time and place. Her love for Jake was here and now. There was no betrayal of Angus in it. It was separate, apart, fixed in its own individual world.

She bathed the boys, as Angela's orders said she should, at a quarter to six, and by six-thirty they were tucked up in bed and drowsily calling for drinks, without any expectation of any materialising. Tony lasted longer than his little brother. He was still mumbling, 'I want some water,' when he finally fell asleep.

Natalie crept into the room and tidied their covers, kissed their warm pink little faces and pushed their teddy bears in beside them before she tiptoed out of the door.

Without much appetite she prepared her own supper and ate it on a tray in front of the television, exhausted by the energy of the two boys. Angela rang at eight and talked excitedly. 'A house goes with the job. We visited it today. There's a sandpit and a swing and three nice bedrooms. I think the boys will like it.'

She seemed to have adjusted, Natalie thought, smiling. 'Have you been interviewed yet?'

Angela laughed. 'Oh, it wasn't like that. We had lunch with the personnel manager and he was a charming man. His wife was very friendly. I'm going shopping with her tomorrow to see what the shops are like over here. There are very good schools within easy driving distance of the house, a play-school for Colin that takes them from three years. Adrian is quite excited about the job, too.'

'I'm glad you're happier,' said Natalie.

'I'm not happy about leaving you,' Angela muttered. 'What on earth will you do when I'm not there?'

Natalie smiled, eyes tender. 'Survive, I suppose.'

'You could always come over,' Angela said very casually, but there was a serious undertone. 'I've asked about the possibility of a job for you and they seemed quite interested when they heard about your job with Metropolis. I'm sure you could get work, a work permit, and until you found an apartment you could live with us. There'll be plenty of room.'

Natalie was touched. 'I'll think about it.'

'I'll find out some more for you,' Angela said with determination, and Natalie saw that she was going to press the idea hard. It would solve her one real problem if she could have Natalie over in the States with her.

'Look after the boys,' Angela said as she rang off. The first moments of her call had, of course, been devoted to a searching enquiry about their welfare and state of mind. Angela was a deeply devoted mother under her brusquely managing mask.

Natalie sat on the couch with her chin in her hands. Going to the States would certainly solve one problem: she would get away from Jake. She closed her eyes on a stab of pain. She didn't want to, of course. It would hurt like hell. But it might be best. Jake was going to hunt her down if she stayed. Sooner or later she would give in to his demands and then she would really begin to know what hell was all about.

That Friday evening when the boys were asleep in bed Jake arrived at the house. She stiffened as she saw him at the door and tried to close it again, but he pushed his way past her into the house. Natalie closed the door and looked coldly at him. 'What do you want?'

He didn't reply, looking her up and down slowly, a mocking smile curving his mouth, and she could have kicked herself for phrasing her question as she had. He was too quick with words, a past master at using them as weapons.

'Please go,' she said coolly, summoning her courage.

'I came to give you an invitation,' he replied, moving away from her towards the sitting-room. She had to follow. She could not leave him to wander around the house as he chose. Impatiently she told him, 'The children are asleep. You must go.'

He stood in the sitting-room glancing around and she looked anxiously at his hard profile. 'What invitation? I don't want to be rude, but please just tell me and then go.'

He gave her no answer, still engaged in looking at the room, and she felt her heart miss a beat as she watched the flicker of the casual grey eyes. 'Please, Jake,' she begged in a shaken tone.

'I like to hear you beg,' he said instantly, swinging round. She fell back, startled. 'You've such a soft, cool little voice, Natalie. I like to hear you pleading like a frightened child.'

She went pale, her blue eyes dark with contempt as she stared back at him. 'You really are unspeakable, aren't you?'

His mouth moved harshly in a mimicry of a smile. 'But you will never again confuse me with any other man, living or dead.'

Her breath caught at the back of her throat. 'No,' she agreed in careful tones. 'No, you make an indelible impression. There couldn't be more than one of you, thank God.'

His eyes flickered, growing very bright. 'Just don't forget it, then,' he drawled, flinging himself casually down on to the couch, his long body stretched out in a half sigh, half yawn. 'God, I'm tired! It's been a hellish week.'

'Work going badly?' She did not want to ask, to be reminded of that other world of hers, but she had no choice. He had brought it with him when he forced his way into the house.

He looked tired, she thought. The hard bones were clenched as though in fatigue, and there were shadows under his eyes, staining the surface of his skin like bruises.

He surveyed her through half-closed lids. 'You're as tranquil as an oasis in a desert. I suppose you've been enjoying yourself all week.'

'I've been working hard.'

'Seeing Tom?' The question was delivered very coolly, his glance moving away from her.

'No,' she said, and he looked at her, bringing a strange hot excitement into her throat.

'I'm hungry,' he said coaxingly.

She sighed. 'I can only do you a mixed grill.'

'Sounds perfect,' he said with a smile that turned her heart over. She went into the kitchen and he followed, watching her cook the meal with lazy interest. She placed the meal before him with a little bang.

'Why don't you eat at the proper times? It can't do you any good.'

'It isn't doing me any good to have you away,' he said, looking at her through his lashes, and Natalie felt herself blushing.

'Did you really have an invitation for me?' she asked as he glanced at her.

'Yes,' he said lazily. 'Your cooking could grow on me. Did you give up your job while you were married to him?'

He never used Angus's name, she realised curiously. 'Yes,' she said. 'He wanted me at home.'

'I bet he did,' he said, head turned aside.

She flushed. 'What invitation?' she pressed.

'My mother would like to have you and the children down for the day tomorrow,' he said lightly. 'Will you come? I'll drive you all. The boys should like a trip to somewhere new, and my mother is dying to meet them. She loves children.'

Natalie was taken aback, tempted to accept yet afraid. Jake saw the hesitation in her eyes and smiled at her. 'I swear I won't jump on you while we're there,' he murmured teasingly. 'My mother is a guarantee of good behaviour, not to mention the two boys. I'm hardly likely to go berserk with sharp-eyed little witnesses around.'

'Well, thank you,' she said slowly. 'I'm sure the boys would enjoy meeting your mother.'

'What time shall I pick you up? Ten o'clock?'

'If you like.'

He drained his coffee and she stood up, expecting him to go, but he merely eyed her consideringly. 'Can't I have another cup? You make very good coffee.'

She poured another cup, wishing he would leave. His presence was a constant irritant.

Picking up the cup, he walked with it through to the sitting-room. She followed nervously, watching the lean tall figure as he stretched on the couch again, arm above his head in a lazy gesture, with every impression of being prepared to stay for hours.

'Have the boys been keeping you busy?' He sipped his coffee, watching her over the rim of the cup.

'Very busy.'

He smiled. 'Angela leave you another of her all-purpose lists?'

She nodded, smiling shyly back.

He gestured with one hand at the couch. 'Sit down. You look like a worried stork standing there brooding over me.'

'You can't stay, Jake,' Natalie told him anxiously.

'Just watch me.'

'Jake, please!'

'What are you going to do about it? Throw me out bodily?' Taunting mockery glittered in his eyes. She was totally helpless to do anything about it if he chose to stay, and he made it clear he knew that.

'I can always ring Tom to come and chuck you out,' she said with defiance.

He lifted one dark brow. 'You think so?' Although he laughed there was a threat in his eyes now and he was not amused, he was angry. 'You can't care twopence for Tom.'

Puzzled, she stared.

'I'll smash him to kingdom come,' he pointed out softly, 'with a great deal of pleasure.'

'Don't underestimate Tom,' she threw back, hating him. He had no right to talk about Tom in that dismissive way, his grey eyes coldly scornful.

'You think I underestimate him? Ring him, then,' Jake invited, and there was derision in his face because he knew he could deal with Tom without any difficulty at all.

She seethed helplessly, knowing she dared not bring Tom into this because Jake would take great pleasure in humiliating him, as he had humiliated her. She stared at him with wide angry eyes and would have given a great deal to have some weapon, any weapon, to use against him.

'Don't you know when you're not wanted?' she burst out at last, and knew as she said it that she had said entirely the wrong thing.

Jake leaned back lazily, smiling, the hard mouth filled with the enjoyment he felt in having been given such a chance to get at her.

'But I am wanted, aren't I, Natalie?' he drawled very softly, laughter in his eyes.

It was the final straw. She dropped her head into her hands with the helpless gesture of a hurt child and began to cry.

He came off the couch and his arms went round her, pushing her head into his shoulder, his fingers rubbing gently into her hair, massaging her scalp.

'Oh, God, why are you such a swine?' she asked him through her sobs.

'Don't,' he murmured, kissing her hair.

'I hate you,' she accused in a muffled voice, her tears soaking his shirt.

'That's better than nothing,' he said oddly, then he lifted her chin and brushed his mouth over her closed, wet lids, over her long lashes. 'You look like a child when you cry,' he whispered, his lips sliding down her tear-stained cheeks. 'A baby. A helpless, desirable baby.' She trembled and he groaned, then he was covering her face with kisses, and her arms went round his neck. She felt his mouth moving hotly over her ears, her neck, her hair, and his arms locked tight around her as though he would never let her go, would fight like a demon to keep her.

'Natalie. Oh, God, Natalie,' he groaned.

She weakly searched for his mouth with a frantic sigh of need, and as she found it closing over her own, a languid wave of desire poured up her body, engulfing her. She clutched at him as if she might fall if he let her go.

The memory of the last time they made love like this faded beyond recapture. Her body was urgently aware of his, her hands moving restlessly over his back, his neck, his shoulders, a burning erotic heat in the long kisses.

'It's no good, Natalie,' he muttered against her mouth. 'I've got to have you. Hungry men are dangerous, didn't your mother tell you that?'

Natalie half laughed, half sobbed, leaning against him with a shiver of submission, and Jake drew away to look at her urgently, making a strange, deep sound in the back of his throat as he took in her yielding weakness, then his hands slid under her body and he lifted her like the child he had called her and carried her out of the room.

CHAPTER NINE

HE laid her on the bed, kneeling beside her, kissing her, breathing faster as Natalie kissed him back without reserve. 'Don't hate me, Jake,' she whispered pleadingly, touching his strong cheekbones with a caressing hand. 'Don't hate me.'

He reared his head in the darkness, staring at her. 'Hate you? My God, what do you mean?'

'I didn't mean to humiliate you that night. I can't go on paying for that for the rest of my life.' She lifted her own head from the pillow and kissed his neck, her face burrowing into him. 'You've hurt me enough now, Jake. Don't hurt me any more.'

She heard the hiss of his indrawn breath, felt the muscles in his throat contract under her mouth. 'Natalie,' he muttered, and then they both heard an unmistakable noise.

Jake swore, sitting upright.

Natalie was off the bed in a second. 'One of the boys,' she said, and then as the high thin wail followed the unpleasant sound of someone being sick, 'Colin! Oh, no!'

She ran into the little bedroom and switched on the bedside night light. Colin was sitting up in his cot, sobbing loudly, his bedlinen ruined. Natalie lifted him into her arms, murmuring soothingly. 'Never mind, darling, Auntie Nat is here. Ssh, you're going to be all right. Poor baby. Ssh!'

Jake walked past her and glanced at the cot with a grimace. 'I'll see to this for you,' he whispered. Deftly he stripped the stained sheets and rolled them into a ball with the top cover.

'There's a linen basket in the bathroom,' she whispered to him as he looked at her enquiringly. 'And clean sheets in the airing cupboard.'

He went out taking the linen with him and Colin's shuddering sobs faded into a whispering. He nuzzled Natalie's shoulder whispering, 'Mummy. Want Mummy.'

'Yes, darling,' she comforted. 'Mummy will come back soon.' Rocking him gently, she carried him into the bathroom, passing Jake on his way back with clean linen.

'I'll remake the cot,' he said.

She hesitated. 'It will have to be washed with disinfectant before he goes back into it. I'll do that after I've washed him and changed his clothes.'

She stripped Colin in the bathroom and he stood shivering, pale-faced and giving an occasional sob, as she washed him. Natalie sank down on to the bathroom stool and lifted him into her lap. She buttoned him back into his clean pyjamas, whispering solace, kissing his little face. 'Poor boy,' she soothed, cuddling him. 'Poor little boy.'

'I see he can take any amount of that,' Jake said drily from the doorway. 'Lucky little boy!'

She flushed, looking up at him, then stood up, carrying Colin. Jake moved to take him from her and Colin turned his face into her with a little murmur of protest. Jake made a wry face.

'Knows what he wants, doesn't he?'

To her amazement she found he had washed the cot already. A strong odour of disinfectant hung on the air and the cot was remade with the clean linen. Natalie tucked Colin back inside the sheets, stroking back his tumbled hair. She knelt beside the cot, watching him restlessly settle back to sleep, singing softly under her breath.

When he had finally slid into sleep she tiptoed out of the dark room and closed the door.

Jake lounged against the wall outside. She looked at him warily, tension in her face.

'I know,' he said drily. 'It turned me off too. I'll see you tomorrow, Natalie.'

She followed him downstairs, searching for a way of telling him she was not coming to see his mother, and he turned at the front door to look at her penetratingly.

'Don't say it,' he muttered.

'What?'

'The thing you're turning over in your mind,' he drawled. 'You are coming tomorrow. No last-minute excuses.'

'Colin may be sickening for something. It often starts with them being sick.'

'We'll see how he is tomorrow,' said Jake. He gave her a strange, mocking little smile. 'Did I say third time lucky? I was out of my mind. I'm beginning to think the gods are against me.'

He went, and Natalie closed the door, sighing heavily. Maybe the gods were against them, she thought. They seemed to move in an eternal circle, never arriving at any fixed point. Tonight she had thought she was lost, finally and for ever lost, but fate had intervened. Now she was torn between relief and anguish. She crouched on the couch in the sitting-room with her face in her hands. There would have been a peculiar and heady delight in giving in to him at last, whatever the consequences. Then she remembered his face as he asked her what she meant by saying he hated her. He had looked stupefied.

Didn't he hate her? Or was it just that he didn't know he hated her?

Could she have been mistaken about his feelings? No, she thought, remembering the violence, the rage, the ice in his face as he sometimes looked at her, remembering the vicious sting with which he had said he would get her one day. How many times he had more or less told her he hated her? He had said he got pleasure from hurting her, that he could become addicted to being cruel to her. What else did that mean but a real hatred?

She went to bed at last, worn out with emotion, and half expected to be woken by Colin again at some time during the night, but he never stirred. When she went in next morning to wake the two boys Colin was sleeping peacefully, his little face flushed and healthy. Natalie looked at him wryly. How typical of children! They were unpredictable, up and down like yo-yos, swinging from apparent death's door to perfect health in a few hours. Thank God, anyway, she thought. It would be terrifying if anything happened to one of the boys while she was in charge of them. Angela would murder her.

She dressed both boys in well-washed blue denim jeans and clean pink shirts, brushed their hair neatly, fed them and sat them down to wait for Jake. He arrived dead on ten and eyed Colin with foreboding.

'How are you today?'

Colin stared with round eyes. 'You're not Uncle Tom.'

Jake's head swivelled to Natalie and she flushed at the look in his eyes. 'No,' he said, glancing back at Colin, 'I am definitely not Uncle Tom. Don't forget that. I don't like being confused with other men.'

Tony jumped down and measured himself against him. 'You're not as big as my daddy.'

'I'm sorry about that,' Jake retorted. 'I'm still growing.'

'So is my daddy,' Colin said.

Tony nodded, giving Jake a satisfied grin.

'God forbid,' Jake said piously. 'What does your mother feed him on? Beanstalks?'

'Are we going?' Natalie asked before Tony could answer that. Jake swung Colin up to his shoulder where the little boy gulped and clutched at his hair defensively.

'Ready,' he said, walking out to the car.

Tony approved of the car. 'Whew!' he exclaimed, bouncing on the springs. 'Great! How fast can it go?'

'How fast do you want it to go?' Jake looked at him perfectly seriously and Tony considered the question.

'A hundred miles an hour.'

'Right,' said Jake, starting the engine.

Natalie's heart came up into her mouth. She sat there tensely as Jake drove through the busy London traffic and out on to the motorway. The speedometer held her eyes. Ever since the crash in which Angus had been killed she had been terrified of speed. She glanced anxiously at Jake. 'Please, don't go too fast,' she whispered.

He gave her a careless grin and the car speed crept up.

'Don't, Jake!' she cried, her hand grabbing his knee.

He looked astonished, then covered her hand with his own. 'Calm down, darling,' he said, and the car speed slowed at once.

Tony complained. 'Go faster, Jake, faster!'

'No,' Jake told him quietly over his shoulder. 'Your auntie doesn't like it.'

Natalie withdrew her hand from his knee and the grey eyes teased her in a sidelong glance, his mouth amused. 'How does Angela like the States?' he asked.

'Very much, it seems. She rings me every night to make sure I haven't neglected either of her precious boys.'

'Is she going to let Adrian take this job?'

'Angela always lets Adrian do what he wants to do.'

'So long as she thinks it's good for him,' he expanded, and she was forced to laugh.

'Well, yes.'

'Your sister should be running this country. It's a waste of her talents for her to be just a wife and mother.'

'Angela doesn't think so,' she returned seriously, and Jake gave her a long, probing look before lapsing into silence.

They arrived at his parents' home and as the car drew up the dogs shot out, barking. Colin shrank, looking nervous, but Tony boastfully announced that he wasn't afraid of dogs. 'Or wolves,' he added with a thoughtful expression. 'Or tigers.'

'Good,' said Jake. 'Because these are wolves, not dogs.'

'They're dogs,' Tony said after a quick look at them.

'How do you know?'

'They're wearing collars,' Tony pointed out, and climbed out of the car, to be swallowed up in a sea of waving tails and licking tongues. A moment later Elizabeth came out in a rose-covered straw hat, smiling and greeting the boys eagerly. 'How nice to see you again, Natalie,' she said, kissing her. 'I wish you'd come again sooner. We kept hoping to see you every weekend.'

Jake gave Natalie a mocking look. 'I told her to come down, but she has other calls on her time.'

She flushed. 'I'm very glad to be here, anyway,' she said, smiling at his mother. 'I hope the boys won't be too much of a nuisance.'

'I'm thrilled to have them. No, I'll take them to have some icecream and orange squash while you and Jake take a walk round the garden.'

'Icecream?' Tony demanded, appearing from under a dog.

'Come along,' Elizabeth invited, smiling at him, taking Colin's hand as she did so.

Jake watched her disappear with the boys and gave Natalie a slow smile. 'We've got our orders,' he murmured.

'I ought to go with them. The boys are quite a handful.'

'My mother can cope.' He took her arm. 'Don't argue, Natalie.'

They walked down through the fragrant rose terraces, the air redolent of that heavy perfume, the summer gilding the garden with the special radiance which only comes infrequently in England but which has no equal in the world and leaves an impression of unforgettable grace on the mind. A faint breeze sighed through the trees. Far below the swimming pool sparkled bright blue in the sunlight.

'You're going to miss your sister when she goes over to the States,' said Jake, pausing to pick one of the pure white roses. He broke off a long-stemmed bud, the delicate petals curled tightly around the hidden fragrant heart. Jake handed it to her casually and she held it, inhaling the scent with a sigh.

'Thank you, it's beautiful.'

'When does Angela go?'

'Quite soon,' she said. 'Adrian goes first and she's settling their affairs here.'

'She won't want to leave you,' he commented.

'She isn't going to,' Natalie said on impulse. 'I'm going too.'

Jake stopped dead. 'What?' He turned a face as white as the rose in her hand, the lines of it as harshly bitten as though he were in sudden agony, his eyes molten with the terrifying violence she had seen in them once or twice before.

'Angela's found me a job over there,' she said nervously.

'No!' Jake shouted hoarsely, and his voice startled some thrushes parading on the lawn. They flew up with an excited twittering.

Natalie stared at him, dumbfounded, and he stared back as if he suddenly did not see her at all, as if he saw something else, something which made him grey and haggard.

He was shaking, as if with a chill, breathing roughly; as though just to draw air down into his lungs hurt them.

'You're not going anywhere,' he ground out, and his words had a slurred incoherence which made him sound drunk. She only just understood them and the look he gave her, the thickness in his voice, alarmed her. Was he ill? she wondered.

She clutched the long stem of the rose and felt a thorn driven into her finger, but barely noticed the pain. 'I can do as I like,' she stammered.

Jake took two steps, his tall, lean body held stiffly, as if he were in constant pain. His hands closed round her upper arm and she winced at the tightness with which he held her.

'I won't let you go. You're not walking out on me.'

Her lips went dry. She moistened them nervously, her head thrown back, the long hair flicking across his hands. 'I'm going, and there's nothing you can do to stop me.'

'I've stood enough,' he muttered. 'I won't take much more, Natalie, I warn you.'

'There's a limit to how far you can push me around,' she flared indignantly. 'You can't dictate what I do!'

His face broke up in violence, the lines of mouth, eyes and cheeks dissolving in a barbaric rage. Dragging her against him, he kissed her bitterly, furiously, and she struggled without success.

At last he lifted his head and she pressed a shaking hand to the hot, aching curve of her mouth.

'Do you think I don't know why you want me to stay?' she accused, the dark blue eyes angry. 'You want to torture me until you feel your ego has been sufficiently placated. I'm going to pay and pay, aren't I, Jake? You hate me....'

'Hate you?' he broke in thickly, staring at her.

'My God, are you blind? I love you!'

She drew a breath which was like a knife in her chest and stared, unable to believe him.

'No!' she whispered, shaking her head.

'God, what do I have to do to show you?' He stared at her restlessly, a dark red coin in each cheek. 'Everyone else knows how I feel about you. You can't be so blind, Natalie.'

'You've been pursuing me to get your own back,' she said slowly. 'You wanted to hurt me.'

'I wanted to do a hell of a lot of things to you,' he said harshly. 'Hurting you was one of them, I'll admit. I'm human. You hurt me more than I could stand when I realised that the night we met you never really saw me at all, just another man.'

'And you hated me for it!'

He laughed without humour. 'Hated you so much I'd have walked barefoot over hot coals to get to your bed.'

'Desire isn't love,' she said flatly. 'You think I don't know your reputation?'

He threw her a brief look. 'Oh, there've been plenty of women in my life from time to time—I'm not an inexperienced boy. But once I'd met you I couldn't see their faces.'

'Anthea?' she prompted coolly.

'You were dating Leyton. Do you think I was going to stand on the sidelines and cheer? Of course I took Anthea out.'

'And slept with her?' She had imagined that from time to time with jealous anger and she needed to know.

'No,' he said, grimacing, and she guessed that Anthea would not have been unwilling. 'I couldn't bring myself to go that far.'

She looked down at the white rosebud which had fallen on the grass during their struggle. Jake had trodden on it and the smooth petals were crushed and discoloured, their sweetness stained. Natalie shivered.

'You deliberately set out to humiliate me,' she reminded him flatly. 'Is that your idea of love?'

'Any ideas I ever had about love went out of the window the night I met you,' he retorted. 'When I turned round and saw you looking at me that night I thought I'd found a walking dream. You looked as though you felt exactly the same way. You came into my arms and I thought you would never leave them. While we danced I was thinking: my God, this is it. I'd always dreamt of finding a girl like you, but as time went by I lost all hope of it. Until that moment.'

She suddenly remembered the gentle passion he had shown her, the melting sweetness of his love-making. Her heart turned over. Was he telling the truth?

'Then my dream come true turned into a nightmare,' he said in a flat harsh voice. 'You stuck a knife in my guts and I went home bleeding to death. God, I was out of my mind that night! Have you any idea what it feels like to think you've found perfection and then discover it was an illusion all the time?'

'I didn't mean to hurt you,' she whispered faintly.

His eyes were brilliant with jealousy. 'Do you think I don't know that? While I was mooning over you like a lovesick boy, you were thinking of another man.' His teeth snapped together, the line of his mouth merciless. 'To my dying day I'll never get over the moment when I heard you use another man's name to me.' He looked at her as he had looked at her so often before, as if he hated her, would like to kill her. 'It had all seemed so beautiful. We went into each other's arms without a word. I didn't even know your name, I hadn't told you mine, because it didn't seem to matter a damn. I knew it was for ever. All that could come later. Just at that moment I thought of nothing but the rightness of having you in my arms.' He rubbed his eyes with one hand as if erasing a memory. 'It hurt so much I could barely speak to you. I was actually afraid I might kill you.'

Natalie stared away across the perfect, close-set flowers in their summer web of leaves, hearing a bee fumble heavily from one bloom to another, the deep droning filling the sleepy summer air.

'I behaved very badly that night, I know that. I didn't want to hurt you, Jake, but I can't apologise for loving Angus. I did love him very much.'

She heard his deep intake of breath. 'Did?' he asked hoarsely.

Natalie looked shyly at him. 'It was another world, another time, and I no longer belong there. I came to realise that.'

He moved nearer, watching her intently. 'I could teach you to love me if you let me, Natalie,' he said unsteadily.

'You can't really make up your mind whether you hate me or love me, Jake, can you? And I don't think I could stand being tortured while you make up your mind.'

He made a fierce gesture, sighing. 'How can I explain? I wanted to hurt you, yes. It was like a disease in my bloodstream, a sickening craving, an addiction. I don't understand it myself. I only know

I was so crazy about you that it hurt every time I looked at you. That's why I persuaded you to work for me. I had to have you around, even though it nagged away like toothache whenever I was with you.'

'You were cruel whenever you got the chance,' she muttered.

'I couldn't help it. It was like making love to you.'

'A twisted sort of lovemaking.'

He grimaced. 'I know. You'd warped the way I felt about you. You'd wrecked my pride that night and I wanted to punish you for it, but above that I still knew I craved for you, a physical need I couldn't stop. And every time I touched you, it got worse, I needed you more.'

'So you want to seduce me to mend your pride!'

'I want anything I can get from you,' Jake said thickly, his eyes passionate. 'I'll take anything— that's how low I've sunk. But I still think I could teach you to love me, Natalie. All I need is the chance. Let me teach you to forget him.'

She looked at him intently, her pale face serious. 'But I don't want to forget him.'

He winced and turned away and she caught his arm. 'Jake, I told you, my life with Angus was in another world, another time. All that's over, but I hope I shall never forget it. It's part of me. It's made me what I am.'

'All right,' he grated harshly, 'I get the message. I don't want it rubbed in, thank you. Hell, you talk about me torturing you! Don't you know what you do to me?'

'Let me finish, please, Jake,' she said gently, her fingers smoothing his sleeve, feeling the warmth of his skin filter into her own.

He bent his dark head, breathing roughly. 'Get it over with, then.'

'The way I felt about Angus was different from the way I feel about you. I thought you were alike, but in many ways you're a totally different man. Angus never hurt me in his life, either deliberately or by accident. From the start, you hurt me all you could.'

She saw his jaw tauten, but he said nothing, his eyes on the grass.

'You set out to handle me roughly,' she told him, half smiling, 'and I hated you for that. Then I realised I didn't hate you any more. I hated to admit it, but I was falling in love with you.'

His head came up and his eyes stared with hungry eagerness at her. 'What?' he asked thickly.

'Hard, Jake,' she said lightly. 'I fell hard. Weeks ago.'

He didn't wait to hear more. His arms were round her and he was kissing her throat, her cheeks, her eyes; his hands tender, whispering hungrily to her, holding her so close she couldn't breathe.

He broke off to look down into her flushed face. 'You mean it?'

'Every word,' she promised, smiling.

'Why didn't you give me a sign? When did you realise?'

'When you kissed me here in the swimming pool. I knew I was physically attracted long before that.' Her blue eyes teased him lightly. 'You knew that, now, didn't you, Jake?'

He grinned. 'I knew I could get you to respond, yes.'

'That bothered me,' she admitted. 'It had taken weeks before I let Angus so much as kiss me. I thought that my odd behaviour that first night was due to the fact that you looked like him, but later I was forced to realise that I wanted *you*.' She caught his grin of satisfaction and eyed him reprovingly. 'Don't grin like that! I was ashamed of myself. I'd never felt like that about a stranger in my life before—I've always been rather shy with men.'

'I'm glad to hear it,' he mocked.

She blushed. 'I think your brutal behaviour had a strange effect on me. I'd been half asleep until you treated me so badly, and you woke me up with a vengeance.'

His eyes flared. 'I hoped I might have that effect,' he murmured. 'I wanted to sting you back to life if I could.'

'You certainly did something to me,' she sighed, giving him a dry glance. 'No man had ever treated me like that before. I was shattered that night you made love to me until I caved in, and then walked out on me. I felt so humiliated.' She put her hands to her hot cheeks. 'It was terrible!'

Jake took her hands away and bent his head, kissing the heated skin gently. 'Darling, forgive me for that. It was a despicable, rotten thing to do. My only excuse is that I was hurt myself and hurt you back to salve my own pride.'

'You really are a swine, Jake,' she said wryly. 'How I ever confused you with Angus I don't know. As time went by, I couldn't see any resemblance at all. I found myself thinking about you all the time. I couldn't get you out of my head.'

'Good,' he grinned, his eyes dancing.

'You may laugh—it wasn't funny. You were on my mind like a tune one can't forget. I began to be jealous of Anthea, to brood about what you were doing when I wasn't with you.'

Jake closed his eyes, his mouth smiling. 'Go on, my darling. I could listen to this all night!'

She laughed. 'I wouldn't admit what was happening until you kissed me the day you brought me to see your mother. Then I had to face it because although I loved Angus very much I had never in my life felt such....' She broke off and he looked at her quickly, his eyes narrow and eager.

'Such what?'

Her passionate look and blush brought his arms round her. 'Oh, God, my darling,' Jake breathed, 'keep looking at me like that.'

Their mouths met, clung, a heated necessity in the movements of their bodies as they pressed together. 'Say it again,' Jake muttered against her mouth.

'I love you.'

'My name. Say my name. I want to be sure you know who I am.'

'Jake,' she laughed gently. 'Jake, I love you very badly.'

'My God,' he groaned, 'I can't wait until we're married—I've had enough frustration to last me a lifetime. If I get a licence tomorrow will you marry me in three days' time?'

Her arms wound round his neck. 'Darling! Yes.' Then she gave a little groan. 'We can't.'

Jake drew away, looking at her with hard anxiety. 'What do you mean, we can't? Natalie, you can't do that to me. You can't change your mind now.'

'Angela,' she moaned.

'What about her? You aren't going with her, that's flat. You're mine, and I won't let you go.'

'No, but, Jake, Angela just won't let me marry

you like that. She'd never forgive me. She's always loved planning things like weddings. She's very good at them.'

'Tough,' Jake said ruthlessly. 'She can plan the first christening. My wedding is my business.'

'But——' she began, and he swept her closer again, kissing her hard, his mouth brutal and hungry.

'My God, do you want to make me go mad? Frustration has been eating away at my insides ever since we first met, and now I'm going to marry you fast before you can change your mind. If we tell anyone they may try to delay things. I'm not waiting any longer than I have to.'

'Your parents,' she cried, horrified.

'They'll understand.' He smiled at her, touching her cheek. 'They've had a very good marriage. I want ours to be like that.'

'Couldn't we just wait a little? A few weeks?'

'No,' he said forcefully. The strong cheekbones tautened. 'Even one week would kill me. I've waited too long already.' He lifted her left hand and stared at Angus's ring. 'I want this off and mine on.'

Natalie looked anxiously at him. 'You won't be jealous, darling?'

'Jealous?' His face darkened. 'I'll try not to be, but if you hear me grinding my teeth in my sleep you must be patient with me.'

She ran her hands up his chest, looking at him tenderly. 'You have nothing to be jealous about, Jake. Not a thing. If you want to marry at once, then we will. I want whatever you want.'

His grey eyes mocked her. 'My God, I hope so. Because you're going to get it anyway.'

Her cheeks burned, but she laughed, leaning

against him, and his face came down on her hair. For a long time there was a core of silence around them. A few loose petals came drifting down with a sigh and lay on the grass like spilt blood.

'Hellcat,' Jake whispered, kissing her hair. 'I've got you. You've made life intolerable ever since we met but at last I've got you, and, oh God, darling, I need you like hell.'

Natalie lifted her face passionately and their mouths clung in a long, hot kiss.

'Daddy kisses Mummy like that,' said an interested voice behind them, and they broke apart, startled.

'Brave Daddy,' Jake murmured, looking at Tony with a broad grin.

Natalie laughed but gave him a reproving shake of the head.

'Aren't you coming in?' Tony asked. 'We're going to have something funny for lunch. It's Spanish and Lizbeth says you like it.'

'Paella,' guessed Jake, smiling. 'Trust my mother to come up with my favourite meal on a day like today!'

'What?' Tony stared at him curiously.

Jake looked at Natalie with such passion that she blushed. 'I'll explain when you're grown up,' he told Tony, then he lifted the boy to his shoulder and carried him laughing into the house.

It was hard to disguise their happiness from his parents. Elizabeth looked from one to the other and smiled, but she tactfully said nothing, although Jake's every word, every look made what was going on very clear to anyone with eyes.

They were married quietly in London five days later. Jake took her away to a tiny cottage on the

Romney Marsh where they had seabirds for neighbours and the whispering grasses hid everything but the sky from them. Natalie was nervous as she went into his arms that first night. At the back of her mind was a secret fear that he would never be able to forget her first marriage, that his jealousy would ruin their love for each other.

Jake held her for a moment, stroking her long hair, his face hidden from her in the dark room. Then he muttered: 'My God, I want you so badly.'

'Jake,' she whispered, trembling.

His fingers stroked her breast and a cry of pleasure broke from her. Her body twisted closer, her arms round his neck. From across the marsh came the low, soft murmur of the sea, but a more powerful rhythm was pounding in her blood. Jake's mouth moved hotly over her bare skin, gentle and unhurried, yet with a growing urgency beneath the slow sensual caresses. Natalie's nails dug suddenly into his back as passion flared deep inside her. 'Jake.' She heard his hoarse murmur of pleasure. 'Darling!' Their bodies merged in a slow possession which held no anger or jealousy, just the silent satisfaction of an overpowering need.

For a few seconds Jake lay still, breathing quickly, as though the mere fact of possessing her were enough, then a wild hunger drove them both, their mouths clinging, and Natalie lost all sense of self in the sensuous explosion that followed.

Afterwards he held her, kissing her hair, and said teasingly, 'You're a very silent lover. All you said was my name now and then.'

'At least that proves I knew who you were,' she teased back, biting his shoulder lightly.

'My God, you'd better,' he muttered, and his hand tightened on her.

'Sated, Jake?' she asked, and he looked down at her blankly.

'What?' She saw he did not remember the threat he had made and reminded him softly.

'I'm sorry, darling. You had me in such a state I sank to making vicious threats I didn't even mean. I love you more than I can tell you, my darling.'

'Show me again,' she invited, and he muttered thickly, 'Try and stop me!'

Before returning to work they drove down to see his parents and give them the news, having already spoken to Natalie's parents on the telephone. Her mother had seemed unsurprised by the news. 'Angela said you liked him,' she said cheerfully, unworried by the abruptness of the marriage. 'I hope you'll be very happy, darling, and luckier this time.'

Jake's parents were equally unsurprised. Indeed, Elizabeth smiled delightedly, hugging them both. 'I'm so glad you finally got there,' she said, and Natalie glanced at Jake in surprise.

He grinned. 'My mother always hears what I'm up to,' he said.

Elizabeth nodded. 'I knew long before I met you that Jake had found *the* girl,' she smiled.

'Did he tell you that?' Natalie asked, wide-eyed.

Elizabeth looked at Jake. 'In his own way.'

Jake flushed slightly.

'He told me you were as beautiful as an angel and you were driving him insane,' Elizabeth said very softly.

Jake's father looked at them all wryly. 'I hope this means we shall be getting grandchildren at last,' he said frankly. 'Jake hasn't exactly hurried to oblige us.'

'Give us time,' Jake said lightly. 'We've barely been married a week.'

'Are you going to work now, Natalie?' Elizabeth asked.

She looked at Jake. 'We haven't discussed it yet.'

'Do you want to?' he asked without expression.

Natalie hesitated. 'That would depend on when you wanted to start a family.'

Jake's eyes glinted. 'We'll discuss this later,' he said, and his parents laughed.

In the later discussion there was no doubt as to Jake's views. 'I want children right away,' he said firmly. Natalie looked at him closely.

'Why, Jake?' She suspected his desire for a family was based on a need to make their marriage as different from her life with Angus as possible and she was not sure she thought it a good thing. It was no basis on which to have children, using them as weapons in a war against a dead man.

But Jake smiled at her easily and said, 'I've always wanted kids. Don't you? And then there's this American offer.'

'What American offer?'

'They've been after me for several years and I wasn't very keen, but when this series is in the bag I think I might take up a contract over there for several years. You'd find it easier to settle down over there if we had children, roots, and Angela would be on hand when you needed her. We'd be in New York, too.'

'That would be wonderful,' she agreed eagerly. Her smile broadened. 'It would soothe Angela down to hear that, as well. She'll hit the roof when she hears we got married without her permission!'

They dropped in to see Angela next morning and she did hit the roof. 'You might have told me! Getting married like that! Not a relative present— I never heard of such a thing!'

'I couldn't wait,' Jake said unashamedly, grinning.

Angela was not amused. She glared at him. 'It was very selfish of the pair of you! Not even telling me!'

'Oh, Angela,' Natalie put in, horrified to see the hurt in her eyes, 'I'm sorry.'

Jake tactfully broke the news of his proposed contract in the States and within five minutes Angela was excitedly planning where they should live and what sort of house they would want.

'As long as it's got a nursery,' Jake murmured.

Angela's brows shot up. 'Good lord,' she exclaimed, staring at Natalie. 'Is that why . . . ?'

'Of course not!' Natalie said indignantly, glaring at Jake, who laughed softly.

'I'm sure we don't have to draw a diagram to explain why we got married so quickly,' he drawled teasingly.

Angela gave him a wry, appreciative look. 'I knew what sort of man you were at first sight,' she nodded. 'I hope my sister knows how to keep you on a chain.'

Jake broke out into laughter. 'Sorry, Angela, the chain isn't going round my neck. I know when to grab a good thing and hold on to it.'

Angela looked with a slight smile at Natalie. 'Yes,' she said, 'she is rather special. Just take care of her.'

'Every minute of her life,' Jake assured her.

Alone with Angela later Natalie waited for her to give the seal of her approval to the marriage, a smile in her eyes. Angela eyed her soberly.

'So I was right. He was irresistible.'

'Entirely,' Natalie agreed.

'How does he feel about Angus?'

Natalie smiled again. Trust Angela to put her finger firmly on the most delicate spot!

'He was jealous, but now I think he's over that.' She smiled more widely, eyes lowered. Yes, she thought. During their honeymoon Jake had finally absorbed her into his own world, their shared world, in which Angus was a memory which could not hurt either of them. At times his lovemaking had been tinged with savagery, a violence which swept her away into total submission, but gradually the hurt had gone out of him and her passionate responses had convinced him that now she loved him and only him.

'Hmm,' Angela muttered. 'Well, if he gets troublesome you can always count on me.'

Natalie repeated that to Jake with a teasing smile later. 'So be careful,' she warned, 'or Angela will get you!'

'I'm shaking in my shoes,' he nodded. 'That sister of yours is a match for ten men. Why she isn't Prime Minister beats me.' He stroked the strands of loose hair lying over his shoulder. 'You do want to have a baby, Natalie?'

'Yes, I do,' she agreed. 'But most of all I want to have a few months alone with you before we start a family. Would you mind that?'

Jake's eyes flared. 'Do you need to ask? Take your own time, my darling. Now I've got you I can wait for the rest of life's prizes.'

She turned into his arms and they kissed deeply, the passionate need growing in both of them at the same rapid rate, their arms tightening around each other.

'Love me, Jake,' she whispered, and he gave a shaken little groan.

'I've done nothing else since the day we met. It will take a lifetime for me to get over the frustration of the months after the party.'

She laughed. 'You've made a start!'

'Wanton,' he muttered, and his mouth closed over her own. The room slowly darkened around them as the evening passed into night, but they never even noticed.

Remember when a good love story made you feel like holding hands?

The wonder of love is timeless.
Once discovered, love remains,
despite the passage of time.
Harlequin brings you stories of
true love, about women the
world over—women like you.

Harlequin Romances
with the
Harlequin magic...

Recapture the sparkle of first
love...relive the joy of true
romance...enjoy these stories
of love today.

Six new novels every month—
wherever paperbacks
are sold.

What readers say about Harlequin Presents

"I feel as if I am in a different world every time I read a Harlequin."
A.T.,* Detroit, Michigan

"Harlequins have been my passport to the world. I have been many places without ever leaving my doorstep."
P.Z., Belvedere, Illinois

"I like Harlequin books because they tell so much about other countries."
N.G., Rouyn, Quebec

"Your books offer a world of knowledge about places and people."
L.J., New Orleans, Louisiana

*Names available on request